"A superbly written, thoroughly captivating novel that is light years beyond the usual one-dimensional crime caper."
—**The Sydney Morning Herald**

"Jan McKemmish's writing talent gladdens my crime-detective fiction addicted heart. From the opening lines (a racy word picture of high summer and low life in Sydney) to the ironic and cryptic ending, her latest novel, *Only Lawyers Dancing*, held my attention. The author directs some well-aimed satiric darts at the private eye/amateur detective genre… *Only Lawyers Dancing* establishes Jan McKemmish as a writer of considerable flair. I look forward to her next novel." —**The Newcastle Herald**

"Different from the rest of the current crop of Aussie crime novels is Jan McKemmish's *Only Lawyers Dancing*. Using literary impulses similar to those employed in her previous post-modernist opus, *A Gap in the Records*, McKemmish takes a critical look at detective fiction, crime and the law that seeks to regulate it, as well as the society these three things reflect. There is continual interaction between the criminal and the law which is as fascinating to watch as an intricate dance—and watch we do, as the lawyers move around McKemmish's crowded dance floor and her book winks at our criminal myths." —**Meanstreets**

"McKemmish relates her tale about old crimes and present-day criminals in a quirky manner by alternating the first person narrative between Smith and Stevens, flickering back and forth between past and present and splicing the narrative with strong visual references to paintings and photographs… The end result is a very impressive novel and probably the most original Australian crime novel to emerge in years. Highly recommended." —**The Canberra Times**

Only Lawyers Dancing

Jan McKemmish

CLEIS
PRESS

Published in the United States by Cleis Press Inc., P.O. Box 8933, Pittsburgh, Pennsylvania 15221, and P.O. Box 14684, San Francisco, California 94114

First published by Angus & Robertson, an imprint of HarperCollins*Publishers*, Sydney, Australia in 1992. This edition is published by arrangement with Angus & Robertson.

Cover design: Pete Ivey
Cover illustration: detail from *Ice* from the series *Redline 7000* by Robyn Stacey. Reproduced courtesy of the artist and the Mori Gallery, Sydney, Australia
Cleis logo art: Juana Alicia

ISBN: 0-939416-70-0 (cloth); 0-939416-69-7 (paper)
Printed in the United States of America
10 9 8 7 6 5 4 3 2 1

Library of Congress Cataloging-in-Publication Data

McKemmish, Jan.
     Only lawyers dancing / Jan McKemmish.
        p.   cm.
     ISBN 0-939416-70-0 (cloth) : $24.95. —
     ISBN 0939416-69-7 (pbk.) : $9.95
     I. Title.
PR9619.3.M325O54   1992
823—dc20   92-46180
                                                    CIP

for the peerless Helen Barnes

PART ONE

Small ghosts

'It's gonna be another hot day in beautiful Sydney, get down to the beach NOW you slugs, you've got a duty to perform here, get out there and lie on the sand for all us inside working fools, it's eight oh five and stea-ea-ming.'

They say it's going to be a hot year: add the El Niño weather pattern to the greenhouse effect, carbon monoxide and dioxide emissions, cattle burps, termite farts and all the human exhalations of silences filled and cacophony. Out at the airport it's hot enough to fry eggs on the tarmac, out west babies are dying of dehydration. In the bush, koalas fall out of trees in their eucalypt delirium. In every scene tourists find exactly what they are looking for from air-conditioned bus windows: Do not go in the water.

The city empties out after the squash of Christmas. There is exhaustion of all the senses. The north coast camping grounds are full, drunken New Year's revelling spills over into murder. Random stabbings. A young man beaten to death to the wild cheers of the crowd. It's going to be a hot year.

This is one of those years called the eighties, every year was called the eighties then, anonymous, waiting, bland-out headlines about interest rates and real estate prices, companies piling profits, and 'rich rules OK' on everyone's lips. You grin at a joke, cool, knowing, you do not laugh. The new rules rule cool, OK. No laughing.

Become a millionaire at twenty-one, skim billions selling hard and fast, buy now, die later.

'What do you want to be when you grow up?'

'I want to be famous.'

There is no real world, no society of hearts and minds, only the surface exists, and close to the surface,

3

beneath the colourful computer images and the magazines full of advertisements and the hundred-dollar diaries that will make you, snap, like that, an executive in anyone's book, beneath the turbo-charged Porsches and the silk suits so suitable in a sub-tropical city, beneath the bubbles of French champagne and despite the shortage of Russian caviar, the old world of the way things have always been is breathing, deep calm breaths of patience and contempt. Ageing bronchial tubes give up cigars and bend to the ears of the new men fronting the neon-light nights of having a really good time.

There are other climates, the old heartbeat of the ocean suburbs, paint peeling and trees bent on the winds, loud talking in the streets, strollers licking ice-creams and eating cakes, overflowing rubbish bins, and whole generations of seagulls raised on chips, no fish. There is the racing blood of the inner suburbs where ageing thinkers read the real estate pages before the book reviews these days, collecting noughts. And then there are the lifeblood suburbs stretching north and south and west to breathe, just breathe.

The city is everything and nothing; it has acquired its own geography, seasons; the air is heated by breathing and machines, bringing the climates of the continent and the ocean to crash overhead, summer storms, months of rain, winters of bright sunshine and that edge of cold from a clear night sky. No frost.

The city is a separate country, floating out from the continent, looking everywhere but there. It is safe, protected. In drought the winters are superb. In flood the rains wash the streets clean into the ocean. In hard times and tragedy the city climbs into the lift and goes express to the fortieth floor. Great view.

After the new year and against all previous weather

4

bureau records, the temperature climbs into the forties and stays there, one of those heatwaves of the fifties, of memory, of the heartbreak way the world used to be. Air-conditioning groans, working to a new pitch of icing interiors and spitting heat into the streets. In bars and cinemas and office blocks the cool air soothes, the hot air rises, creating a vacuum. Breathing becomes difficult. Bodies slow to half pace and faces take on the pale blanched mask of sweat and dry, sweat and dry. For days the urge to panic hovers in the haze. Rain drops on the pavement as big as footprints. Clouds mass and break, lightning strikes, adrenalin races. Sweat and wet, pores open, the city moves up to jogging pace, resumes.

CHAPTER 1

1. ARRIVING AT SPEECH

Being part of this, driving into work early to miss the midday heat, to meet a new client. Excited. The guy has a history, a long history, and I'm up and coming, on the make, and driving easily into the city with the headlines and the inside information. Radio glides from disco beat to hip talk, 'This is the big city sound-and-issues station bringing you the latest in grooves and news.' Voices over music, the latest technique, a familiar voice, there she is, in fast-art-radio-mid-sentence I struggle to disentangle.

'. . . it's not a violent image . . . it's symbolic . . . I like to work with people in trouble, they have such good faces, you can study them . . . like a book . . .'

This is Frances Smith, I'm sure of it, turn up the volume. A rush of old friendship and rediscovery, she is here, in this city, somewhere. I pay attention. Frances Smith takes photographs. Or that's what she was doing when I knew her last. In Melbourne. In the seventies. Taking photographs. Moving around.

I come down through Double Bay and lose the drift in the tunnel under Kings Cross, the static comes up with the carbon monoxide levels and by the time I'm out into William Street, breathing sun-raddled air with the best of them, she's gone and the music is pounding from my Datsun like a hoon cruising on Saturday night. I leave the volume up high and laugh. It's ten past eight and I'm running late. The information comes at the end of the track. '. . . Smith has caused a stir in the Sydney Festival this year. Her photographic study has been labelled rabid feminism rearing its ugly man-hating head . . .'

I note the location, a gallery in a warehouse down the Rocks. I'll have to pay it a visit or send a postcard saying something like 'No publicity is bad publicity' or 'Even the attack is blatantly phallic'. I settle on this last one going up in the lift of a building in Macquarie Street. In such places even the fantasy of subversion seems brave.

First-up a meeting with the new client, one of our big-time big-name chaps, a respectable crim. He's late. He's cancelled. I could have slept in, missed the radio notes and perhaps the rest of the story. Coincidence. For a few years life was like that. For a few years everybody's life is like that.

That year my life was like that. Frances Smith stepped into it. Peripheral. A voice on a radio in the Eastern Suburbs peak hour. I could have let it go, like I'd let a lot of the past go, off into a blur of missed meanings and deal-with-later files. I had a lot of baggage. Everyone has a lot of baggage. Smith and I went a long way back, and the cancelled appointment gave me time to think

Frances Smith and I grew up in neighbouring towns outside Melbourne in the 1950s and 60s. Essential rural childhoods changing into suburbia as the city spread to envelop. We weren't best friends as children. We knew who we each were, me the policeman's daughter and she the daughter of the famous Smiths. We met up as young adults in the city where everyone was assumed urban, middle class, educated, free. Perhaps it was that neither of us were these things that brought us together. Occasional friends at first, we became closer, talking long into the night. Even that could have been transitory but for the coinciding biographies, geography, class, and the opposing but always connected sides of the moral fence. Backgrounds that mark you one way or another, and for a while — seven years — I worked as a therapist and backgrounds were my business.

Later, I turned to the law; at the time it seemed a logical step. Many clients in therapy had been damaged by legal and illegal abuses, fraud, state intervention. I was tired of dealing with the damage, treating the wounds and seeing the system perform its rightful stuff with the perpetrators heroic, media stars, great copy, the victims feeding our ravenous appetites, vicarious and glad, us not them. I became a lawyer to 'defend the rights of the damaged, the powerless'. There are worse reasons.

I have made good money, acquired a certain reputation for thoroughness and toughness. I am not in danger of being deluded. I work for anyone these days and take the cases as they come. That is the way the system works. I work within the system.

I'm due in court at ten and buy the postcard on the way, Sydney Harbour from the air, a tireless view. I feel good in my soul as I walk the short block to the court building, confer with the client, check his story against the brief. We are asking for an adjournment. I go into an appeal at eleven. After lunch I'm in conference with the QC I am briefing in a major case scheduled to resume next week. This appointment, the looking forward to this meeting, makes the day exciting.

I spend the lunch hour at the Festival Exhibition and look about for Frances, find the controversial photograph — one small image of faces in a mirror, a woman watching a man shave. Above her out-of-mirror head is a thought bubble with the same in-mirror photograph but this time the man's face and throat are cut, sliced almost, and bleeding freely.

What disturbs me about this set of images is that the people, the subjects of the photograph, are middle-aged and old-fashioned, they are 'good, upright people' from the past. Her hair is in a confection of curls at the front and cleaved into a french roll at the back. He is balding, wears a button-down shirt, a thin tie across his shoulders ready for tying. The bathroom walls are 'tiled' with that fifties-style tileboard. He is shaving with an authentic Wilkinson Sword safety razor. You can almost smell the Palmolive shaving soap. And the mirror is square, a shaving mirror, but with those fussy bevelled edges. At the side of the photograph is the title: 'Mum and Dad prepare for a night out, 1965.'

I deliver my postcard,

liked your work, let's see each
other while you're in town, I'm
in the book, Watsons Bay.
Anne Stevens

and walk back through the tourist traffic to the office, sunshine blue sky, warm and muggy. I am almost too relaxed for the conference, which goes well into the evening. The case has turned difficult — new forensic evidence favours the defence. We are prosecuting and it's a national case, the full bit, press in every edition. I go home to work the notes into submission. Frances Smith calls at around ten.

'Can I come out and see you?' she asks.

'I'd like that,' I say. 'When?'

'Tomorrow, I guess, I'm only in town for a few more days.'

We make a time and I give her the address and she

says, 'That's so far out,' and I say, 'You take the number 370 bus. It leaves town at seven-fifteen. I'll meet you at the terminus.'

Watsons Bay is far away from the city but close to the ocean. It's a tiny place of tiny houses and a tiny beach and all that tininess is dissolved by the ocean crashing through the heads, the rangy bush up the cliffs at the back of the two or three streets and the fabulous views west towards the city, the sunsets, all that walking out along the headlands, the Heads, blasted by ocean, winds and oxygen, The Gap.

What I really like about The Gap is that this city can even institutionalise suicide. The Gap is a great scenic tourist place where you can go when it all gets too much and feel the last wind in your face, on your skin, and all the trouble of the world, the whole continent, is at your back. You might climb up and brace yourself against the fence and then, when the moment is right, lean forward and fall. Suicides do not jump. They fall out into the air and tumble slowly over and over, disoriented, in some unimaginable bliss of consciousness, until the moment of impact. Splat. That's that. I always think of The Gap as a civilised arrangement and of the tourists as somehow humanised by their bizarre pilgrimage to this place: get out of the bus, walk along the track, take the photo, look east and south and north and west. It's not an ordinary moment, it's not an ordinary view. This might be what they have come halfway across the globe for. Quickly now, back in the bus, on to the next thing. Tourists never jump, or fall, but they might be aware that leaning into the air and looking towards death happens here, like anywhere else. It is accommodated, allowed for. We are a society familiar with death.

2. IMPARTIAL IDEAS

I wait for Frances Smith to arrive the next evening. Max Cavanagh, the cancelled appointment of the day before, has telephoned for a new time. My secretary, Deidre McSweeny — efficient, unservile, a real slave-driver — has written him in for eight o'clock the next morning. I skim the files again.

Max Cavanagh is not a stranger. While Australia has been embracing 'the eighties' — in pursuit of pure capitalism, having a riotous time, people on buses talking in millions and billions as if they are familiar — somehow, almost without us noticing, the everyday business of crims and crimes has become big news. Anyone with more than a passable living from the paralegal has had their name in the papers a few times, repetitiously captioned, alleged this and reputed that. That's how I know Max Cavanagh. He's a tabloid filler, a blurred photograph, a name that echoes fear in hearts. Like many of my clients, he'll have a they-done-me-wrong story and I will ask only those questions that can be answered with the truth.

I also knew Max Cavanagh from legal gossip. And criminal lawyers more than anyone love to gossip. Gossip is their lifeblood, their relief from the terminal boredom of the unfictional courtroom or the days in the office. It is their lubrication, their juice, their balm at the end of another day of putting some poor bastard away for the crime of being caught. I am curious and a bit hungry.

The papers have had one or two blurred photographs of Max Cavanagh lately — head and shoulders, slightly cadaverous, perhaps handsome, never looking straight at the camera. And they've had the usual lines: rumoured, reputed, alleged to be an enforcer for Mr X or a numbers man for Party Y. The newspaper files tell me he's been tried and acquitted of murder, conspiracy, illegal gambling and assault. He has contacts. He has protection. Why does he want to see me? I am small change, a solicitor working the scene, on the way up. I am working hard, but not in the big league. I am curious, not frightened. A bit scared and a bit interested. I want to play this game, shout drinks after a big trial, win or lose, call on the remotely attractive senior partner for advice late at night, weary, worried, grateful for a good brandy. But beyond the dreams I'm not sure I want Cavanagh and his implied worlds or the real thing: big business, big money, big lurid stories of shotguns fired by men at their own heads because the alternative, the verbally described alternative, is too much for the stomach.

I go down to meet the eight- and nine-fifteen buses. No Frances Smith. She arrives at the house well after eleven and I am surly. We haven't seen each other in three years. It is too intimate, too focused on the people we had been years before. I am tired, have drunk too much coffee. She is all wired-up and ready for the big reunion. I should have stuck her in the spare room and skipped the memories. But living alone in the suburbs does strange things even to those who choose it. I put the kettle on and place the bottle of brandy on the table. I open a new packet of cigarettes and turn the late-night jazz on the radio down low. I want something, still, despite my careful crisp edges. Intimacy. The talk of old years. Something. I gave and got more than I bargained for.

3. Two

I collect Anne Stevens' postcard in my routine cruise of

12

the desk at the exhibition. It surprises me but I take it and read it like a cool cucumber in a perfectly tossed salad. More signs. Sydney is like this. Invitations out of the blue, old friends in tasteful suburbs, a night out near the ocean — someone tell me I am dreaming.

I am here for the Festival Exhibition which I am almost painfully grateful to be a part of. And I know I'm going to stay. There's no question. Here I am in a city that wants to exhibit my work. Well, one photograph, I know, and an old one, one from my student days, but there's something large and breathing about a place that allows.

The exhibitors' meeting goes on and on. We have to put out a statement about censorship and trite reviews and art and society. I want to be involved; I am the subject, after all. But I find the discussion so similar to every other meeting I have been at that I can almost guess who will stand up next and claim a global perspective while speaking entirely from the heart or the stomach or the ego. I drift off, first in a daydream of a large exhibition all to myself, then into real sleep. When I wake up the gallery is an emptied room and although I can hear voices — confiding and confident, erudite and critical — somewhere off behind the partitions, I cannot find my way to them and end up outside in the soft warm air that wraps me in its arms and I walk up through the city and wait and wait at the wrong bus stop and then find the right one and so arrive. I find the house, one of three tiny weatherboard cottages in a row in a side street, each with glimpses of the water and attic rooms that promise more and soft yellow lights in the front windows. They look, ancient, quaint, containing. I knock. We are awkward with each other. I am shocked. I hadn't thought about it. I stare at her as she buzzes around making tea and setting out the glasses for the brandy she assumes we will drink.

I'll spare you the reminiscences, interesting though they are to me and her. There is a point to the telling of this story, this meeting of old friends in a new city, this night of radio chat, art, geography, the social, and alcohol. It was a long night, with a breath of breeze and salt in the air and the two of us by fast turns, wary and distant, assuming and intimate. We did 'I remember when I first met you' and 'great friendship resides in difference and distance . . .' and then we fell into the real, a conversation I may have heard echoes of over the years but, coming as it did in this still quiet night in a strange city from a woman I had known half my life, it seemed both new and familiar, visiting the past for the sake of the visiting.

4. IT'S THE HUMIDITY

'Remember the Newman–Green murders?' Anne Stevens said this night. 'When they happened I was sent away to boarding school. They happened ten miles away from where we lived.'

She says, 'A lot of people knew more than they were saying. I remember phone calls late at night, cars roaring up to the front gate, my mother furious and worried and trying not to weep, pushing us into the back bedroom as someone or some people stood in the front hallway and talked in loud voices.'

I say, 'Yeah, I remember that, every time we went into Staunton in the fruit season the police would pull us over and check our licences and search the car. We stopped going after a while. It was too heavy.'

14

Stevens continues her story oblivious to my response. 'When I came back from school for the Christmas holidays a year later we went off to midnight mass. It was Christmas Eve and I remember being excited. It was late at night and I was grown up, sixteen, dressed up in my city clothes, overdressed of course, seeing people I hadn't seen all year, and it was sticky, humid, which was unusual for that place of dry summers. We all glistened with sweat and saw everything through a haze. We sat in a row in a pew, mum and dad on either end, my two younger brothers and me in between, candles, music, the smell of incense.'

'A religious experience,' I say, wanting to cut through this romantic nostalgia for the rural. I was scathing about the fashion for misty reminiscences, brittle about rural conservatism and ruthless about the effects of mythologies on the present. But this night I was failing, couldn't raise an argument. Anne Stevens simply talked on as if I hadn't spoken.

'Another family came and filled up the rest of the pew. I remember we had to move our bums, to squash along and dad was on their end, and me next to dad, then the two boys and mum. We always sat in that order in church. It was a matter of some undefined pride that I sat beside my father, in the privileged position, although it was probably because I behaved whereas the boys fiddled and dropped things. Later I would realise how we, mum and I, always contained them in public so dad could appear as the benevolent master of us all. It was important to him as a policeman, so often seen as threatening.

'That night in church there was a still moment, the voices of the choir ceased, the priest stood with his back to the congregation and my father, standing at the end of the hymn, began to shake and shudder and sob. The priest sort of twitched, everyone looked from the slight noise and movement to the priest, he turned slowly and continued the mass as if nothing was occurring and my father sank down, shaking, sort of blubbering silently. I sat staring straight ahead. My mother couldn't see anything from where she was and I knew she wasn't aware. Later she said she didn't realise, nor the boys. The family on the other side, a pale man, a smaller cowering woman, a girl, a boy, all seemed to me that night to be pale and stringy-haired.

'In that full church past midnight with the greatness of adolescence and beauty and sensibility upon me and a new frock and a light suntan over my pale freckles and my hair all long and full and curling, I stood and mouthed the responses and stepped past my now silent father and left him there for the altar and the priest and the blood and body of Christ.

'It's difficult, still, for me to talk about that time. I have glossed the days with re-writing and analysis and layers of meaning and significance and the sort of spoken versions of family tragedies that carry more pathos than truth. And there was so much unspoken, unknown, that we made up entirely other versions for the various purposes, for family, close family, friends, colleagues, the force, the doctors. In this way, in the public speech in the sitting room over cups of tea and too-sweet sponge cake, we overheard each other speak and did not need to tell each other anything.

'The priest came at lunch-time on Christmas day. The boys had been given their presents and sent out into the street. I was busy cooking, carrying on as if nothing had happened. Dad was in the office at the front of the house, sitting, as I suppose he had been all night, with a brandy bottle, staring at pieces of paper.'

5. AN OLD MURDER

When it's late in the night and the talk has become important I know not to push. I was tired. It wasn't her story, it wasn't my story and what I remember from those times, what I could say about them, didn't fit in this night of disturbing memories spoken out loud. I collected the clean sheets and said goodnight, cleaned my teeth and climbed into the attic to look out the window with the moon, hear the water, feel the breeze. 'The new city whispers its promise and I'm going to take it,' I said to myself, and 'It's an old story, the new is always gripped by the past. Loosen up.'

I stretched with exhaustion and relief, a brief moment of security, thanks mate, I could smell the morning coffee, guaranteed to be real.

The fragments of that gothic night came out one afternoon when the clouds massed from the south and that strange green light that, Stevens said, 'presages a change in our lives', painted the western sky in place of sunset. And we waited, tense, entirely present, part of the place and its weather of grand drama, for the great thunder and lightning storm to come in and charge us with responsibility for all things. 'So we could' — Anne Stevens again — 'face the task at hand.' Then, returning to the material, like Madam Mao on a good day, 'I wonder if the verandah is leaking.'

She has a pompous side to her that can irritate. It used to irritate me, now I just laugh. There are perfect moments when eeriness makes for plain telling, when the present is the present and doesn't stand for something else. Sometimes, in these green sky times, things are exactly what they seem.

Anne Stevens said: 'I dreamt about my first lover last night. I can't recall the details, the plot, just that he was there. All that going back provokes these uncertain dreams. It's not a coincidence, or a symbol. He was there at the time. He brought me a present on Boxing Day, a great garish box of soaps and powders and perfumes. 'As if I smelled terrible,' I said to mum. She said I was too hard on him. She quite liked him, even though he wasn't a Catholic. He wrote me a letter a week for the whole of my matriculation year and I was . . . grateful, I suppose, that he had stuck with me despite what had happened.'

'What *had* happened? For God's sake, Stevens, are you going to tell me the rest of the story or indulge yourself for hours again? I'm fed up with all this family stuff. I bet it turns out that it was all the mother's fault.'

I summarise the hours of telling: Anne Stevens' father had a nervous breakdown in midnight mass. It was precipitated by a terrible vision, a prescient moment, a smell, the odour of a particular sweat that lingered, chemicals combined on particular clothes in particular proximity. It was an unusually humid night.

Graham Newman and Stella Green were found murdered in January 1965. They were bound and mutilated, sexually assaulted, beaten up, left to die in a patch of bush out along the old Staunton road.

When the bodies were discovered Arthur Stevens had been the first policeman at the scene and he had set up the cordons and placed blankets over the terrible sight and stood back and waited for the homicide blokes to arrive. He had kept a good watch, quiet, brushing away the flies rhythmically and replacing his hands behind his back, shifting his weight on his carefully set-apart feet. Looking, looking, imagining the scene as it was, as it might have been, layer by layer, shape by shape, colour by shade of colour, meaning. As a painter would, breathing the still cool air as it became a warm morning and then hot, the full heat of a summer day. Early January. The murders tainted the whole season but the hot summer morning, something, the drying dew on the earth, the shifting air in the leaves, something must have given off a smell, a sense of the ones who had done this.

No-one was ever charged although there were many rumours and later full-blown myths: a respectable man who covered his tracks with threats and favours, protecting his sons, some said, or his mates. And the unexplained violence, the very viciousness of the crime, entered the fabric of the community.

The public version laid blame everywhere: bikies, Queenslanders, fruit-pickers, roadworkers. Bloody itinerants, the locals reckoned, keeping themselves safe with notions of dangerous strangers.

I say, 'We remember different things and we remember things differently.'

Those murders touched me where it hurt most — in my social life. I was allowed to drive into Staunton on Saturday nights with the only young men dad trusted with me, Rudi and Damien, fruit-pickers down from Queensland for the season, vaguely thirty-ish and the sons of German migrants. My father is Frank Smith. (Yes I was named after him. 'Can't single out one son to carry on my work,' he'd say by way of splendid explanation. 'They'll all be in it equally, but my little girl, she can have the name, she's special, my special girl.'

Mother would smile. Her name was Joyce and I was really pleased to have missed that.)

Frank Smith had taken a liking to these young men and their little Volkswagen car and their cleaned-up-for-a-night-on-the-town shirts and ties. Their European maturity was one factor but really I suspect he liked them because they had nothing at all to do with him or his work. They were straight, good men who came down for the fruit season and worked hard and were saving up to buy houses for their chosen brides. And they would take me to the pictures or a rock dance and watch over me as I had my fun.

After the murders, every time we went out in their car the police pulled us up and checked papers and asked questions and wanted to telephone my father. When I said my father was Frank Smith they'd calm down and let us pass but it got wearing after the third or fourth time and we took to playing cards and records down at the pickers' huts, drinking beer from cans, with me smoking cigarettes and badgering Rudi and Damien to tell me what the real world was like. They wouldn't. They were well brought up polite men who worked hard and saved their money and went back up to Queensland when the fruit season was over. A year or two after the murders they stopped coming and I had to be satisfied with family social events. Then we moved into the city and everything changed.

I stayed out at Watsons Bay with Anne Stevens for a week before finding my own place, closer in. Redfern, a friendly household used to interstate visitors, a room high in the roof with a view west over the railway tracks. Peace and no quiet. The way I liked it. I hadn't thought about the murders since that time. I have my own reasons for forgetting. And I have my own set of images of the past. A set of photographs, carefully arranged.

SLIDE:

Here is a photograph, one of the first I took: age fifteen; year, 1965; place, Karella East, thirty miles north of Staunton. The occasion: my first camera and a Boxing Day fair. I have thirty or so from the same roll of film, all described in a kind way as 'arty'. Clown faces in rows and fat ladies with fairy floss.

This one is of the Le Garde twins — a country rock duet. They really were twins. Here they are out the back of the tent after a performance, tired and beery in their fringed white suits and their gleaming red and gold guitars. That's my mother in the background, looking away towards the rest of the family who are out of shot. She's wearing gloves and a hat, a crisp dust coat and low-heeled shoes to match. She looked that day like a matron of the community and I remember being proud to walk with her and that we laughed a lot and had fun and she won a silver horse on the knock-down stalls and gave it me because I wanted it so much.

I show this to Anne Stevens and say, 'This is what it's like, this is what kids remember, not the other stuff, the deep and dark and definitely meaningful. I think you're dredging this old well of memories for motives in the present. How is your father these days? Is he still alive?'

CHAPTER 2

1. THE MAX FACTOR

I leave my car for Frances Smith to use. She's moving into a house in Redfern. I'm not entirely pleased about this. Perhaps if I'd known she was going to stay around, even if she is ten miles across the suburbs and in another world of art and inner-city concerns, I wouldn't have spoken so long and freely about these subterranean things that seem to have come back to haunt me.

In the early seventies I worked in a clinic for a few years — community health, family therapy, mixed-up kids and battered wives, lots of alcoholics and an increasing number of addicts. I know the grip and the release, the process of fixation, self-deception, self-awareness. I still practise these techniques. It is useful in legal work, extracting and remembering details, playing out hunches about lies and truth, watching, waiting, letting things go on until something revelatory is spoken. And now Frances Smith, old friend and handy listener, recipient, catalyst, is staying around, a telephone call away. These spontaneous acts disturb my careful life.

So I take the bus into town. It is very calming. I arrive at work clear and brisk, in mid-stride. Max Cavanagh comes in right on time, impeccably dressed. He shakes my hand firmly and waits for me to sit down.

'Pleased to meet you, Miss Stevens. You know who I am. You got the right papers?'

I nod, listening carefully to the slight nervousness in his voice. 'Why don't you tell me your situation?

This is not my normal line of work.'

'I'll be frank, Miss Stevens,' he says, and I resist the temptation to say 'What's wrong with Max, Max?' or 'I doubt it'. He continues, 'I do a lot of work for a lot of different people. You don't have to know any of that. Some crusading cop reckons he can nail a couple of murders on me. This is the first one.' He throws the press cuttings across the desk. I leave them there.

'I don't believe everything I read in the papers, Mr Cavanagh. The arrest warrant specifies one George Jones, cause of death — multiple blows to the head, incinerated corpse, no smoke in the lungs, three years ago. Affidavits from certain informers. Unnamed so far. It doesn't look like much of a case.'

'I know, I know. Some guy in the nick was offered release in exchange. It's happening every day. But I don't even want it to go that far. I'm, well, let me put it this way, like a lot of entrepreneurs I make my contracts on the basis of good will, reputation. George Jones was a popular guy, left a wife and three kids. That wasn't a nice job.'

'Not your normal style?' I can't resist the barb. This is all looking like a con job with me as some sort of clean front. 'I'm not sure I want my reputation blurred by this nonsense either, Mr Cavanagh. Why don't you go to your regular lawyers?'

He stares straight at me. 'These things are a formality, Miss Stevens. It's not sensible for me to defend myself in court, though I could. I'll work out all the angles for you; you're just there to please the judge. That's the deal. You don't have to get your hands dirty.'

I flip the switch in the tape recorder with my left foot. We all use them these days, entranced by the technology, and by the danger. A Supreme Court judge had gone down on illegal telephone tapes a few years back. We want our own records, every word might have to be counted. Cavanagh smiled; he'd heard the click or had a sixth sense, so I asked my question. 'Who's trying to get you, Mr Cavanagh, these "cases", what is it now, one every six months? You might have a lot of enemies but this level of litigation is ridiculous.'

'It's these new straight cops, they're scared not to. They go by a different book.'

'Someone's supplying them with information.'

'There are lags everywhere if the price is right.'

'Witnesses against you aren't known for their longevity —'

'I win in court.'

'These days?'

I weary of the patter. He is a master of it but even he is starting to look genuinely weary. At fifty-odd years and after his sort of life he probably should look a lot worse. His skin is smooth, a clean shave from a barber this morning. He's kept himself fit and lean. He is easy in his body. We sit in silence for a while. I want to offer him a drink, and have one myself. 'Conspiracy to murder,' I begin, 'is a very serious charge Mr Cavanagh. You'll have to have more than an alibi and a — '

'Destroy the witnesses in the box, Miss Stevens. You have a certain reputation for that. They've all got priors and the jury will be impressed that a woman would defend me. I'm always frank, Miss Stevens, and I expect you to manage this. It might not do much for your reputation but then again, I'm not exactly small change. Your colleagues will tell you how generous I can be. And there's always the future. I can offer a certain amount of protection if ever you need it . . . In your line of business there's always some punk who doesn't see the system as a lottery, like we do. '

There it was. The threat. I knew it would come, but hard eyes and cruel mouths don't come up on a voice tape. I reach for his file and we go through the details until the phone rings for my next appointment. It is only nine a.m. and I am still wanting that drink. We shake hands again and say *au revoir*, I pencil his name in my diary for the following week, eight-thirty a.m. precisely, and know it will be changed by the afternoon.

2. THE FATHER

My father was pensioned out of the police force in 1969. I'd left school by then, free and off to university, a new world. My mother and father stayed on in Karella until the boys finished school and then they moved to the coast, a little weatherboard house a few streets back from the sea, tea-tree scrub out the back, a big garden. Mum played golf, and joined all the local things — church, cards, book club and historical society. My father spent the days in the garden and the nights playing patience until the TV screen went blank. He became silent, shuffling, dreamy for most of the time and weeping in brief spasms on certain days, when the north winds came.

When my mother died, suddenly, quickly, he seemed to rally, said he could look after himself and did, making a big production out of shopping and cooking and managing on the pension. He even sent me money when, at the age of thirty, I gave up counselling, moved to Sydney and went back to university.

The money he sent me was small in amount but large in importance. It kept the reliable pleasures of movies and eating out in my schedule. And it was, for me, a mark of his approval, despite his verbal contempt for the entire legal profession. 'A bunch of sharks,' he'd mutter, or 'Charlatans the lot of them,' or, most often, 'No better than the men they defend.'

My father was not a saint. He was a country cop with all the necessary handy opinions about town bikes and blackfellas out on the river and doctors who made house calls on young widows. It was a country town; the boys drove fast and got killed, the girls either left or became pregnant or married. Once he'd had to put three or four local boys into reform school for a gang-bang. That was hard. There was a lot of pressure to let them go. As usual. Most of his time was spent with drivers' licences, gun licences, shooting permits, keeping an eye on the pub out on the highway, speeding tickets, accidents, bereavement, stray stock on the road. He called the Staunton crowd when anything big happened.

The Newman–Green murders had shocked him. My mother rather disliked him for it. Having a weak husband ruined her place in the community. I was more sympathetic. It seemed a sort of noble thing to me, so far away, safely in Melbourne and deep into psychology textbooks.

These days we have a telephone relationship. Whenever I get into trouble, am made weary by the awfulness of a case or my own mistakes and incompetence, or just troubled by some unspecific alarm, I phone him.

I phoned him. 'Hello, hello, Dad? It's me. Me, Anne. How are you? I'm fine. Yes. It's OK, you know, working hard. How are you getting on? Oh yes, yes, really, oh, did she? And what did Aunt Joan say? Have you talked to her? Oh. What hospital is she in? I'll send her

26

a card. Did you? Mary was there? Mary who? Oh. How was she? Really? A chauffeur. For a businessman. Very smart. Does she wear a uniform? Of course not. A car phone? Of course. She'll be able to be in constant contact with the hospital. In the city. That's a good thing. That'll be nice for her.

'Where did you stay? Out at the house? The old house? Where's that? No I don't know, Dad. You're talking about these people and I don't even know them. I've never . . . you don't talk about them, Dad. You haven't. I don't remember. I don't remember that. They came to visit once when we were children and I took Mary tree-climbing and she got stuck and we had to call the fire brigade to get her down. There was a photograph. It used to be on the shelf at the top of your wardrobe. Of course I looked up there. I was a kid. There was the shotgun, yes I know, I never touched it, and the photograph of Uncle Alan and Aunt Joan, married 1941 and a long letter from him to you which I read but probably didn't understand. Later there was another photograph of Uncle Alan and a different woman and two babies sitting under a tree in some godforsaken place, a park in Perth, with the sea glaring in the background, a colour photo, a snapshot, and the woman was wearing a sundress, white with strawberries or cherries on it and the babies were lying on a rush mat on the grass in playsuits and the man and the woman were drinking from wine glasses, I remember that distinctly because I'd never seen wine glasses before.

'Dad?

'Look, I should be going. I just rang up to see how you're getting on. Yes. No. I'm fine, I'm just working really hard at the moment. Sometimes I'd really like to talk to you about some of the stuff I'm doing. Of course you would. No. Mostly drug cases and assaults, armed robberies and stuff, you know. You used to say a crim is a bloke who's stupid or unlucky, he's the one who gets caught. Well, I reckon luck's not a factor, some of these guys are really stupid. I mean, they watch TV or read the papers or whatever and go out wearing a gun or a knife and they make with the one-liners and suddenly the stick doesn't play his role or the lights go out or there's someone in the queue at the bank before him with a hold-up note and he just stands there in the line watching the guy load the money and thinks 'ah ha'. In the movies Mel Gibson'd walk out with the stranger–robber and they'd become buddies and go halves in a beautiful outlaw story, riding off into the sunset in a Porsche. But instead the guy races out with the successful bank robber who sees him as one of those general public heroes and shoots him in the street and the guy just lies there bleeding and crying and saying "But I was on your side," and gets done by the cops as an accomplice accidentally shot by his buddy. I mean, it would make you weep wouldn't it Dad?

'Yeah. He got five years with three and a ruptured spleen and a punctured lung and waiting two years to come to trial and the guy's literally a broken man. I mean, he's twenty-three or something and does fifty push-ups a day and doesn't smoke and talks about gaol like they do in the movies but Jesus, yes I know, sorry Dad, he's . . .

'Sorry.

'Of course it worries me. Of course it's only a job. I know. It's a game. You always said that "Lawyers are the fat kid at the birthday party, no matter how shitty the other kids are to him he still gets the biggest piece of cake". I know. I'll ring you again next week. OK, maybe I'll come down for a weekend soon . . . OK. Bye Dad, keep well, bye.'

3. HISTRIONIC HISTORY

Anne Stevens arrives home in a terrible temper. I make myself scarce, pack up my few belongings in readiness for tomorrow's departure and take a walk along the harbour until I figure she'll have calmed down. I return to a sizzling meal and a sort of farewell evening. She says, 'I rang my father today. I don't know why I do it, what I expect of him. We always fight, he always has a go at me.'

I stare at her. 'Of course you know why you had a fight with him.'

She stares back at me. 'What?'

'All the time I've been here you've been obsessed with those damn murders and the overblown meaning of it all, bloody church and hymns and daddy's nervous breakdown.'

'I . . . I suppose . . . I suppose I want to punish him for . . . what? Failing? No. It's not that. He didn't fail.'

'I think you don't much like some of the things you do these days.'

'And?'

'And, you take it out on him because you think he's better than you are.'

'Oh.'

'You've defended rapists. This guy Cavanagh sounds like he's had more than his share of justice.'

'OK. OK. Yes. In the short term, I can see it, I can see it, but, but . . .'

'But there's more to it than that. You don't want to

be so simplistic. None of us do. In this position of departing guest, a welcome but disturbing friend, I will acquiesce,' I say, 'I will listen. What else have you got?'

She goes to the kitchen and opens another bottle of wine. I make social in-fill to bridge the gap between one story and the next: 'People in Sydney drink such a lot. They strike me as Americans. But then, this is a convenience. Everyone in Australia drinks a lot; perhaps in Sydney you notice it more because there is so much else to do.'

'Or so much more to forget.'

'Trash histrionics, my dear. Perhaps Sydney *is* like America: you both take yourself too seriously.' That's a leading line if ever I heard one. She takes it up.

'The last time I went to visit my father we had a long long talk. Well, I did all the talking, he listened, nodded and agreed in all the right places. I told him about a woman I had seen a few times at the Community Health Centre.'

4. LILY SPEAKING

Lily told her story backwards. I had a feeling it had been told several times before. I made notes. I rarely made notes while a client was in the room. I was trained to work my memory, not total recall, but to use what the memory gave back. But Lily's monologue was different. There was an element of revisiting somewhere that had ceased to exist and a sort of desperation that it be true, that it had been true, that it had been, like this, this simple, this clear.

'I got into, dope, smack, oh, six months after I went back up to Sydney.'

This was nothing new. Everyone was into the risks.

It wasn't crime. It was lifestyle. It was business and everyone knew how to make the deals, though even the great addicts from Melbourne were shocked at the scale.

'We went back up to Sydney for Christmas, 1981 I think. Joey was restless. We drove up overnight and headed straight for the beach. The sun was full up and we swam out past the breakers and floated on our backs and looked out to sea and back to the shore. We stayed out at the beach for a week or so. It was like a honeymoon. Joey'd go off in the afternoon and phone me around eight and I'd get dressed and ready and we'd go out for the night to a little club on Pittwater and he'd play at the tables and I'd lean over the roulette wheel and sometimes win.

'This night we drove into town all dressed up, Joey in a dinner suit he'd got from somewhere, borrowed from some guy he'd met, a tuxedo I guess. And I had this long emerald sequined blouse and a tight black skirt and high, high heels, just like Sue Ellen in 'Dallas'.

'I felt great. We sang in the car and crossed the bridge with the radio up loud and the lights of the city. "Like in the movies," Joey said, "it's gonna be grand."

'Robert was at the blackjack table. Joey pointed him out to me and sat at the side table to wait for him. Robert Simms, short, handsome too, and so smartly dressed he seemed to shine, to glow. I thought: he's dusted with gold.

'Ruth came and sat with us. I'd known her from when I worked in Sydney before but she wasn't surprised to see me and Joey together. Joseph she called him, and Robert called him Jo Jo. They hugged and clasped hands and forearms. Robert turned to me and took my hand. "Lily you look beautiful," he said, as if continuing a conversation from the day before, not at all as if we'd just met for the first time.

'Ruth took over the conversation, as if there was a script to be followed. I remember that she was telling me that Robert had great plans for Joseph. "Now that he is back 'with us'," she said, as if he'd been ill or lost presumed dead. She said how she was sure I'd be glad to be back in Sydney. "Melbourne is so dreary, isn't it?" she said, and I just sat there looking and smiling and smiling and wondering why none of it felt any good at all. I blurted out, "No, I mean, I quite liked it, it's so flat and calm and blue," stuttering like a fool or a girl, repeating myself, stupidly, "I really liked it, we had a nice flat . . ."

'And then I could hear my voice, high and girlish and I knew then, because I've been like that before and I know what it means — that I was in danger, I was trapped, I was being made into someone else for some-one else's reasons and there was to be no argument. There was no way I could stop my voice going shrill and rising at the ends of the sentences and Robert and Ruth smiled and nodded at each other and Joe was rubbing his hands together and looking around the room ready for some action and I went on and on in my high voice to Ruth as she shepherded me towards the ladies room and we powdered our noses, people still did that, and I blurted out to her how really it was great to be back especially as Joey and I well, could she tell, coy as all hell and playing the lines like I had invented them, back near the family and all, as well, could she tell, I was going to have a baby.

'"Not pregnant. Don't tell them you're pregnant," Joey had been absolutely fierce. "Tell them we're gonna have a kid, that's that, no pregnancy that can be dealt with. This is a kid, my kid and we're having him."

'"OK baby, fine. I like kids, I want kids," but I knew what he meant. I'd been fixed up twice already, it was dead easy, easier than saying I love you and I'll look after you. To tell you the truth I was surprised Joey was so keen. He'd always moved around a lot. I knew he had other girlfriends, even when we lived together, but maybe he did love me or something, or maybe, yeah, sure, jeez, I'm so dumb, he was scared, then, going back to Sydney, getting back into the game as he called it. A wife, a kid, that's real, that's normal, that's not so easy to disappear.

'When I'd said "Collingwood" Ruth had grimaced. But I was serious. "It was lovely," I said, "the top half of a house, right down on the river, very quiet and lots of trees, almost like the country," I said, and realised at that moment it had been a hideout.

'Things really changed then. I was looked after I can tell you. I had three babies in three years. I started to work again, not the game, no siree, not any more, I'd got out of that for good. I went to work for Robert Simms and Andrew Williams; they were partners then. I had an office and a secretary and someone to mind the children. I got smart, studied bookkeeping, the tax laws, real estate. Robert and I used to have a meeting every week. I was desperate to impress him, used to swot up a sweat before every one. Then we started doing lunch. That was fine. Sometimes Joey and Ruth would come along and we'd make a night of it. Sometimes just Robert and I . . . He educated me you see, he wanted me to be . . . and I wanted to be . . . Joey was bored with the business side. He was more active, physical. He loved being with the kids, especially as they got older. And he loved making deals and contacts, setting up "situations", as he called them, "making a few calls". I knew what that meant, flying out on the last plane, gone for days or weeks.

'We went back to Melbourne, you know. Rest and recreation, Robert said, but I knew Joey was too hot and we had to split. Did a midnight flit. Put the kids in the car and headed out through the mountains, taking the backroads to the border. We settled back into the flat and Joey took off — business as usual, I guess. I put the kids in school and made a go of being the proper mother with dinner on the table at six. He was never there to eat it.

'The second rape happened here in Melbourne. In the flat, with the kids asleep in the next room. I was too scared to make a sound. It's had a terrible effect on me. That's why I came to see you, somebody. I can't shake the fear. I know you'll probably think I should be able to handle it. I've been a prostitute, I live with a hired thug. But it's terrifying me.'

'Did you go to the police?' I asked, sure beforehand that the answer would be no. It was. She grinned at me and asked what kind of psychiatrist I thought I was. I said I was a counsellor trained in therapeutic methods and she got up to leave. I said, 'You don't need another psychiatrist, you need to go to the police. I'll come with you if you like. They'll at least take a statement. It's not just you, you know, it's all the other women he might do it to.'

She glared at me then. 'Other women, who cares?' she said. 'I've got this bloody hex on me and you want me to have a social conscience. The cops'll probably give me the same again. Thanks doll. You're a real winner.'

Despite this more than accurate attack she came back four times for an hour, over several months. She would ring a day ahead to make an appointment and arrive exactly on time and walk in through the door and push her sunglasses up onto her head and sit down in the chair across the desk from me. She would turn half towards the window, looking off into the distance and showing me a three-quarter profile. She would talk. I would comment occasionally. She would stop mid-sentence when I looked at my watch, rise to go, collect her bag, sort through it for keys that were always in her pocket, for sunglasses that were always pushed up on top of her head, find them both, pack everything back into her bag. The minutes ticked past. I usually turned away to do something else, waving a goodbye dismissively as she completed her production. 'The credits are rolling,' I said one time, and she kept on walking.

I liked the edge of style she could bring to my small plain room in the Community Health Centre where I rarely had a chance to make a difference. And she wasn't afraid of the ambivalence. She knew she'd been raped, that she was a random victim, that her life, her life with Joey, was ambiguous in relation to male violence. And she refused, by coming to see me, to be an isolated victim. I guess I liked that sense of power she had about her. She was really strong.

We did go to the police eventually. The second rape was one of those random terrorist attacks certain men make on any and all women. The police took her statement. They allowed me to sit in on all their questioning. We were both impressed by their professionalism. They said they had a file, several attacks in the same area over several years. They'd get him eventually. I think it made her feel more at ease with the whole thing. She came back one more time, I think, but she was changed, tense, distrustful. Joey was back in town; they were heading for Sydney at the end of the month. 'Thanks for your time,' she said. 'I guess it helped.'

5. WHAT DID LILY LOOK LIKE?

We come up out of the reverie of other people's stories and I want to ask 'What did Lily look like?' and 'How did your father respond?' but I can see that these details are not the point. Stevens is held by the difference of the narrative, the echoes of Max Cavanagh's world in this long-ago tale told to a bystander. Not involved.

'It's a coincidence,' I say. 'You must come across this sort of thing all the time.'

We look into the deep blue night of a long summer evening. It's not even late but we seem to have come to the end of something.

'What did Lily look like?' I ask, trying to push ordinary reality through the vicarious identification that is going on, doctor with patient, lawyer with client. The intensity is seductive. The difference, the otherness, is a classic case. I start to feel nauseous.

'She looked like an ordinary mum who had walked in off the streets on the off-chance, you know — the kids were in school and these places had been set up by the government so she might as well see what they had to offer. She had good auburn hair, thick, not dyed, pale skin, the sort that freckles but doesn't tan. She wore one of those track-suit suits that were becoming leisure fashion items around that time, blue with a yellow trim. She carried a fabulous leather carry bag, always, great bottomless thing, as if she might at any

36

moment be required to live from it for an indefinite period of time. She was tallish, not short I mean, slim and a bit wiry. She had on those fashion tennis shoes, runners, but I had the feeling these weren't her usual clothes. She didn't look at home in them.

'On her last visit she wore a suit, hound's-tooth pattern, tiny checks with a black velvet collar. The sort of thing I rather like, good cut, good fabric, and smart low-heeled shoes, every inch the business woman in the city or madam out for a day shopping and lunching with a stack of credit cards and a taxi home with all her satisfying parcels. She was always playing a role.'

The phone rang and I went to do the dishes, my last perfect-guest gesture. The moon out the kitchen window and I listened to the deep silence of living right out here on the edge of the ocean. I was going into town with Stevens first thing in the morning. I hadn't climbed the cliffs or visited the famous Gap. But I'd done my duty as receiver of disturbing thoughts and sounding board for worried Anne and her determinedly done big job in town. Now I was off to start my own life again. The people I was moving in with were impressed by my recent newspaper notoriety. They'd learn. Fame isn't witty dinner table conversation and a constant round of fascinating phone calls. They'd see. I spend half my life in small dark rooms with the radio and dangerous chemicals for company.

SLIDE:

Here is a photograph I took while I was in Watsons Bay — the view from Stevens' front window. A sliver of sea glistens in the distance. A haze of people drink and eat on the foreshore. And there, just there, Stevens is walking briskly out of the crowd, head up, briefcase in one hand, bottle of wine in the other, coming up the street from the bus stop, high summer 1987, just before the world revved its motor and drove fast towards anyone in its way.

CHAPTER 3

1. NEWSPAPER INTIMACY

For those first months I lived in Sydney it was always summer, the blissful blue sky days of February going March and melting into April as if winter would never happen. The heat was full all day and the nights stretched on longer than the heart could bear. You can always tell a migrant first arrived in this city: we get drunk on the weather and the soft warm nights full of imminence, taking the promise of the place on trust, striding off into the streets with the slightly off-centre confidence a native would never reveal.

To the permanents, those who had been here six months or all their lives, cool reigned. And I mean crisp, icy, every sentence uttered inflected down at the end. Extraneous adverbs rampant. Really. Actually. Honestly.

'Do you really want to go and see a movie tonight?'

'Do you actually believe you can make a living from photography?'

'Are you honestly going to live in Redfern?'

'Honestly? Maybe. Maybe not. What's honest when the starting point of a society is trying it on and getting away with it?'

Anne Stevens and I are supposed to be going to see a movie but something has come up. Stevens is in full flight to my new house-mates in the lounge room when I come downstairs.

'Look at this.' She thrusts a newspaper into my hand as I walk in. I look.

'Hit man missing. Rumours rife in underworld. Police search for body.' I look at the headlines and the

39

blurred photo of a familiar face. Joey Simms. I've been here before. I look at Stevens. She is wild-eyed, keyed up, and for a moment I think it is because I am late again and we will miss the ads at the movie. But then I see that she is actually upset, really worried, honestly disturbed.

'Do you know him?' I ask.

'No, not him, his wife. Read the paragraph on page two.'

I do that: Lily of the psychiatrist's couch. The rape victim. The classic crime story. I read:

> Lily Simms, wife of well-known hit man Joseph (Joe) Simms, said today that she believed her husband had been killed. She wept as reporters pressed her to reveal more, then faced the cameras squarely with the promise: 'I'll be seeking representation at the inquest.'

And I turn back to the front page with the blurred photograph:

> Police are investigating reports that well-known hit man Joseph Simms has been 'rubbed out' by rivals in Sydney's current gangland power struggle. Information received suggests that Simms was killed on or around the night of March 19 and his body dumped at sea.
>
> Joseph Simms is the brother of well-known Sydney businessman Robert Simms who was not available for comment.
>
> Joseph Simms is alleged to have been responsible for a number of recent gangland-style executions including the shotgun murder of Stan Phelan outside his Woollahra home and the beating and burning of

George Jones, whose remains were found in the boot of a stolen car in the Ku-ring-gai Chase National Park on New Year's Eve.

'That's why I don't read newspapers,' I say, not to her in particular. It's true, I don't read newspapers because too many people I know might feature in them. My father, the brothers, the uncles. I'm a Smith. Frances Smith, daughter of the infamous Frank Smith, alleged Mr Big of the Victorian underworld. Rich, flamboyant, popular, well-liked, generous, honourable, a multi-faceted business entrepreneur. These days he's very respectable and never mentioned in the tabloids; his domain is the business pages, the sports pages, the race track and takeover strategies. One of those exemplary self-made men.

There is no mention of Mr Smith and his past connection with Joe Simms. That was years ago now, old news, obsolete scandal. Dad always liked a likeable young thug on his way up and Joe Simms was definitely likeable. But his disappearance looked like a local matter, inefficient work practices perhaps, or redundancy, services no longer required. That's the trouble with being a hit man, my father would say, it's a small business, success means you attract takeover bids or dirty tricks, industrial sabotage. On some deep philosophical plane you are always killing yourself slowly.

'It's inevitable,' my father would say, 'but you can't tell them that, they want the job. It's the one job everyone fantasises about, the highest an individual can go, great fear, enormous power, the ultimate, and respect, always respect. You can't tell the young blokes. I used to say, "Show me a retired hit man," and they couldn't.

"Name one," I'd say, "who was had a proper funeral."
The big silence. They always think they'll be the first or
maybe they don't care, maybe the whole thing is made
possible by some absence of the nerve endings that
connect fact with fact. But there's nothing like a good
killer either. Or a good kill, they tell me.'

2. The empty house

The empty house I craved and organised echoes. I make
coffee — it goes cold, I cook dinner I can't eat, go to
bed blissfully early and am still reading at four in the
morning.

House guests take up so much time and I always
miss them when they go. And the telephone doesn't
ring. I go in to work early and leave late. I work back
three nights in a row. Cavanagh's hearing is a week
away and I'm so prepared I could do it blindfold.

The boy I represent today has a can of spiked coke
tucked in his sports bag. He's on tranquillisers and is
up for armed robbery. Very slowed down. A big lad,
thatched blond hair and wearing sunglasses indoors.
He moves and speaks slowly, as if someone has hit him
hard and many times about the head. He minds his
manners and tries to conduct an ordinary conversation
with me as we wait for his name to be called. He sips
from the can of coke smelling of whisky, says: 'I should
have been born earlier, gone into the army, that would
have given me a chance to do something with my life.
Could have gone to 'Nam.'

He lives with his mother. He's very sorry. He can't
remember. He wishes he hadn't done it. Or he wishes
he hadn't got caught.

He takes out his Walkman and puts it on, listening

to his collection of seventies desperado cowboy rock tapes. 'They had great music in the seventies,' he says, 'not like Triple J. They're full of communists.' He keeps losing his umbrella on the bus and making slow steady inquiries about getting it back. He's twenty-one and his brain is gone. He can't get a job.

The judge and I steer him towards counselling, detox. He has legal prescriptions for Serepax, Mogadon and Rohypnol from several doctors. His mother wants to pay me in cash straight away. I ask her to wait until I send the bill at the end of the month.

After he hears 'suspended sentence' he feels a lot better, says 'I was shit-scared of going to gaol.' He doesn't hear probation, or bond, or in the custody of his mother. He drains the can of coke and takes another pill, grins at me, takes off his dark glasses. Very formal. 'Thank you Miss . . . I hope I won't be seeing you again,' he says, with a small 'nothing personal' laugh.

I am back in the office by one o'clock. Cavanagh rings. He wants to see me. Something's come up. I can't say no. I say OK. He says six o'clock at the Regent coffee shop. I say here or nowhere, mate, I'll see you at six. I put the phone down very gently. It's a try-on. Something very fake in the delivery. Of course he doesn't show. It's a game but what sort? I think of pin the tail on the donkey but it's too cute. Golf perhaps. I feel like the tee right now. Stuck neck deep in dirt and waiting for someone to take a swing. It's just Friday afternoon. And still no word from Harry.

3. LE BAR

Anne Stevens rings me late Friday afternoon and we go to see the movie we missed the week before. It is her choice, but I am easily persuaded — *White Nights* with Mikhail Baryshnikov and Geoffrey Hines. It's an awful Cold War crass plastic tear-jerker but Baryshnikov dances on celluloid and that's why we and the rest of the audience come. It leaves a sour taste in our mouths, complicit with the ideology machine. America can turn anyone into an anti-Soviet mouthpiece. Somehow this diminishing of the world leaves us depressed with ourselves.

We go up to the Cross to make contact with the real. Le Bar is one of Stevens' favourite places and new to me. It has a bar at one end, a small stage at the other and ten or so tables with chairs. It's surprisingly ordinary. The clientele are ordinary. There are no stiff vertical hairstyles or pouting lipsticked mouths, no boys in shiny suits smoking cigarettes like death threats against the wall. We find a table and are joined by a man and woman — Solange and Anthony. Anne Stevens introduces her friends and her mood changes and we are suddenly talking about the rumours around town as if we all know everybody and have the inside information.

Someone called Wendy gets up on the stage, all six inches of it, and sings clear clean blues with a slide guitarist and I am in heaven. When I return to the table conversation Stevens is telling Solange and Anthony about Lily. I half listen. The whole vicarious soap opera's gone stale for me in the presence of a voice and a cadence, a broken note and a held-back wail on a steel guitar. I'm a sucker for the art. I buy everyone a double whisky and the barmaid asks me if I'm new in town. I nod and take the drinks back to the table. The talk is going on. I lean towards them, just a little. The night turns again.

Stevens is saying, 'Lily Simms didn't make any more appointments and I didn't take on another patient in her place. She rang me last week, out of the blue, said she'd seen my name in the papers occasionally, kept track. I am in the phone book. She rang me at home and we went for coffee. She talked about the latest chapter in the story — Joey's disappearance, his supposed death. She was sure. It was as if she thought I was still her therapist.

'I suppose his girlfriend and his killer will come to the service. There won't be a funeral — "Can't have a funeral without a body, luv" — so we'll have this creepy memorial service in an Anglican church and everyone will make serious speeches and then we'll all go to Robert's place. Joey was *his* brother after all, not my boy.

'And I'll enjoy that. Robert's got one of those million-dollar mansions down on the harbour, you wouldn't know it was there from the street, all trees and triple garages. We'll stand around out on the terrace and the lawn. There'll be polite sandwiches and French champagne of course. It was Joey's favourite drink; he thought that was how the rich lived. Joey would have loved it.

'You know, that second rape, when we were in Melbourne, just before I came to see you that first time. It really threw me. The thing is, I was respectable now, middle-aged, middle class, a proper mum, in my own home, the children asleep in the next room. I couldn't tell anyone.

'And I knew him. Not knew as a friend or anything, no name, but I recognised him, I'd seen him before, a long long time ago.'

'As a child?' I suggested.

'No.'

'Tell me about your childhood.' I pursued the clue.

'No. It's not relevant. I want to deal with this, now, what I've told you.'

'Joey's death?' I asked, 'Do you want me to represent you?'

Lily looked appalled.

'I am a lawyer, you know that, so what exactly do you want?' I said to her and you know she just got up and left. Disappeared into the Double Bay crowd. I mean, what did she want of me, what did she expect? Stevens pauses. Solange and Anthony pay attention to the shocking double scotches. I try to rescue the conversation and the evening, 'Lily Simms sounds like one hell of a dame. Looks like you'll be getting plenty of work if you keep up that contact.'

Stevens slumps into her chair. Solange glares at me with disapproval, Anthony pats Anne's hand and says, 'It's OK sweetie, don't take any notice of your friend. She's new in town. She doesn't understand the implications.'

I laugh at them all cowering before the high seriousness of real crime. The barmaid collects our empty glasses and I suggest another round. No-one declines and no-one goes to collect them. I do. When I get back the talk is all about Tina Turner and the possibility of her appearing at Le Bar when she's next in town. I tune in. I'm a Tina Turner fan from way back. We resume the fantasy of having a good time and they leave in a group after the next drink. I stay for Wendy's last bracket and am rewarded by an influx of fans who don't know me from a bar of soap. Anonymous, safe, no longer new to the city.

4. Love

Anne Stevens met Harry in a Kings Cross bar one night. He was an ex-everything and beautiful in a battered sort of way and he laughed at her.

Harry Bean was a battered man, sun wind acne football car accidents and a few years as a bouncer in his misspent youth meant his face was a moonscape and his body a map of the world. Anne Stevens thought he'd be just the rough romance she was looking for and was shocked to find him dropping her at her front doorstep, a shake of the hand, and a 'keep your head down when the guns start,' enigmatic goodbye. He'd called her bluff, he had her number, he'd seen right through her streetwise pose to the core of her bourgeois soul and its sexual fantasies of muscles without brains.

He came by two Saturdays later, midday, she opened the door to his knock, stared. He said, 'Yes that is a gun in my pocket but I'm on my lunch break. They say the fish and chip shop down the road's not bad.'

She wanted to say, 'I'm pleased to see you,' but her corn wasn't as clever as his and it committed her to something his had neatly invoked and avoided.

Harry was working as a semi-permanent extra, fisherman, bartender, body in the dark, in a film and the whole crew was at Doyles. Great seafood platters and jugs of beer and wine. Cast and crew mixed together, it was the end of the location shoot on the surrounding cliffs and in the mock house they had built over weeks on the headland above the beach. I'd read the book and had felt a proprietary interest in both film and book — it was being made in my suburb after all. The director was praising Harry's grace on the dance floor in the wedding reception scene. The bridesmaid, an up-and-coming actress, was clearly torn between an interest in Harry and the attractions of the leading man. Star quality won out and Harry walked me up along the cliff top to the set for a look, he said, at how reality is built on illusions.

He hadn't read the book and for the first time I felt at least on an equal footing. 'It's a great novel of illusions and the frauds romantic love plays on the condition of women and desire,' I said. 'It captures the perfection of poverty and struggle, colonial states, Australian times, the necessity of flight, fleeing, following, going on knowing the wanting is wrong.'

'Does it have a happy ending?'

'Of course.'

'Do you believe it?'

'I believe in the art of it. The satisfaction of the sentence. The language.'

'I've got to pull this thing down now,' he said. 'I'm staying on as demolition expert, a man of many talents.'

'You should have let me say that.'

'You don't know enough about me to throw lines around.'

'And you know all about me?'

'Enough.'

'I'm not even trouble?'

'Do you want to be? I've given up saving maidens.'

'No. Or maybe. I know what I want.'

'Good. I like that in people. As long as it's real. What they want. Not a lot, red roses at sunset and duelling pistols at dawn, great soundtrack, Lou Reed and Midnight Oil pounding meaning into meaning.

'You've seen too many dawns. I like the blues played with clarinet and saxophone, a duet pure and percussionless, after midnight, out by the sea, listening to the waves pound the cliffs, very elemental, the edge of the city.'

'Take care,' he called as I walked off over the cliff tops, to home, the car, getting out of here. 'Shit' — a noun.

SLIDE:

Here is a picture of pure envy. Me — Frances Smith — glowering at the camera after Anne Stevens and I had a bottle of wine for Saturday lunch and she told me she'd sat next to Sam Neill at lunch the day before and didn't know who he was.

That's her place in the background. The French doors opening onto the balcony, the dregs of a bread and cheese repast. You can see past the house to South Head. The air there, above the ocean, is always, always lucid.

Chapter 4

1. Little ghosts

I am reluctant to speak about the past. My reluctance, and it is an almost physical resistance — the lips won't speak, the body in continuous motion, doing every little thing: the washing, the gardening, the shopping, hustling for work, three jobs at once, no time to think, deadlines, excuses, extensions, exhaustion, a sort of heroic urban existence that feeds on the very images it works to produce, reproduce. I am not a photographer by accident. Non-verbal, solitary, little dark rooms, cosy chemicals, darkness and light, that place where the real is all manipulation.

I can travel backwards as long as it's fast, glimpses of events and faces, a few lines of conversation, a certain place, the way the wind was that day.

I lived in Melbourne in the seventies with half a dozen people, a big house, the perfect distance provided by high-density intimacy. I came into the house one afternoon to find two motorcycle cops in the lounge room, hands on guns on hips. They were looking at the radical posters stuck on the walls. When I asked what they were doing there they asked if I knew who owned the Holden ute outside and I went out and looked at it and said no and why and they said they followed it across the freeway, one like that was used in an armed hold-up earlier in the day, and do you always leave your house open?

I invited them to sit down and went up through the rest of the house and found Betty drinking a can of beer in her room. There was an air of someone just gone. Downstairs I told the police I had just gone upstairs to check and there was no-one else at home. They left easily with a last look at the 'Keep warm this winter, make trouble' poster that had the university in flames. Betty came downstairs with the can of beer in her hand and I said, 'Where is he?' and she replied, 'He's in the wardrobe,' and I said, 'What's he doing here?' and she said, 'I like him, we were having a beer,' and I said, 'I don't want any crims or dealers around here, I can't afford it,' and she said, 'OK, don't get so uptight, he's a nice guy and he sure has good dope,' and I said, 'Yeah, let's roll a joint,' because the cops had gone and Joe's dope was always first class and he was a nice guy in his own way and I felt, here, in this large house with a thousand people and the posters on the walls, protected, safe at least, part of the ordinary discourse between crims and politics, the middle class and the times.

It was a strange loop in my life story. I didn't feel calm or easy or safe with my father. With him I was definite. His world was so dangerous you had to leave it. Like my mother left it, in horror.

This is one version of Joe Simms: neighbourhood drug dealer, delivering on time and always top quality, lover of Betty Brown, university student radical, feminist and nice girl from Beaumaris. One day she'd work for the UN and later she would write quite good small novels but for now she was dabbling in the underworld and I had to agree that Joe Simms was very handy at parties. He kept the gatecrashers out and the dope smoking.

I didn't know then as I know now that there was a wife across town and a career of classic proportions in the making, although I didn't like the look of Betty Brown when she came back from the lost weekends out of town with bruised blue eye sockets and a new fashion for long-sleeved shirts. She moved out a few weeks after I asked her if she was all right and she said just fine in that superior early-junkie way. I let her go. I'd seen it all before, I didn't want to know.

I didn't want to know a lot of things that I knew. Life is like that I suppose but I did want to tell Anne Stevens. She was working the criminal law scene and not knowing that it wasn't like on TV.

'That's crap,' she said, mindreader she. 'I know what's going on, I see it every day. You think I think these people are beautiful lost causes to be redeemed by my brilliant defence strategies?'

'Yes you do. But you can't get involved.'

'I don't,' she says, 'No dough no show. It's a tough world out there. But it's tougher inside, they say.'

2. JOEY SIMMS

Years before this but before during and after the Joe and Lily show, there were a heap of stories of the young Joe Simms starting out. One went like this:

Joey left Sydney for the first time when he was fifteen, a kid on the move and heading for 'the life', as he would say, 'money, action and power, freedom'. This was in the sixties, and he meant something different from the hippies.

That was clear the night he and a couple of mates, fresh out of Pentridge from a car-stealing and a couple of assaults, were drinking at the pub when some fool invited the bar to a party up in Carlton.

Joey and his boys stayed on drinking and muttering a random refrain, 'Fucking Carlton, full of communists and hippies, women without tits and blokes without balls, university types drinking coffee and thinking they're living.'

As they walked up through the city they found themselves outside the house of the party and started to smile. Then they were in the house pushing along the downstairs corridor and out the back into the kitchen. They handed beers from the fridge, saying nothing and listening to the fabulous talk around them. Upstairs, music, rooms crowded with people, a man wearing glitter on his eyes — young, decadent, clear-skinned. Someone was passing a joint, a thin discreet joint, and no-one was paying attention. They were laughing, smiling, dancing, great blues on the stereo and then something hot, fast. Joey recognised it from some Sydney summer night of long ago — Lou Reed.

His smile became glassy, steely. One mate had his hand on a woman's arm and she was turning away from him and talking to someone else. The bloke with glitter on his eyelids began to dance with her. You could see the fear before they even felt it. Another bloke, big, looked like he could fight, walking up to Joey and offering him a beer. Joey swung. One punch and the room went into slow motion. Joey pulled a knife as the big bloke came back at him. He did know how to fight. And one of the mates had a gun in his hand, just there. Like a toy, one of the panicking women would think. And Joe and the mates moved back to back to back in the centre of the room and laughed and hooted as the room screamed 'leave him alone' and 'don't shoot', like a bunch of school kids. Joey snarled and lunged at the man with the glitter face, slicing him across the cheek. Slow motion as the blood oozed, then shock and silence and noise occurred all at once and people were going over the balcony and the big guy was trying to talk reason and streetwise and the three guys ran out with arms full of handbags and were gone into the night.

Back at mate Mark's place, they turned the bags over and raked a meagre fifty bucks together and a load of Drum tobacco and address books and contraceptive pill packets. Mark's sister Sandy took a new hairbrush and helped herself to the best leatherwork and they threw the rest out the car window as they drove across the city to Johnny's Green Room with a flask of whisky and a long night for playing pool.

A night or two later some jerk had his throat cut in downtown Lygon Street. It was after the pubs closed and Joey and Mark and Stevo had been awake for forty-eight hours. The whisky was still tasting sweet and they headed out along Sydney Road in a brand-new Falcon, passing the Pentridge gaol in careful silence and turning off to Broadmeadows to collect the cash for the job.

Joey could do that. Drink. No sleep. He was coolest when the blood was flowing. He'd spent the night drinking with the guy, faking camaraderie and making plans. This guy could introduce him to people, he had connections. Joey's pure young face and smiling blue eyes, deep blue, not washed out pale blue like Mark's, not evil, not cruel, looked back at the comrade with eagerness, gratitude. 'Yeah could ya, I really need a break right now.' He was meeting the guy's eyes, calling him Mr and hunching his shoulders down into his chest — the beaten kid. The comrade bought beer by the jug and tried to cut Mark and Stevo out of the round. 'Fucking glass eyes,' he said to Mark, reckoning on his power over these punks, a man with a reputation, connections, something they wanted, he reckoned.

They reeled out of the pub way past closing time and Mark and Joey faked a fight with each other and Mr Comrade stepped in to claim his boy Joey. The boy slipped behind him, grabbed him by the hair and pulled the knife across his throat, fast, walking quickly around the corner, sprinting for the car, quiet now, exhilarated by the work, the neatness. A paid hit made to look like a drunken brawl.

They drove through the dark and the dawn until they crossed the border into New South Wales. The sun was hot and high in the flat dry country and they pulled up by the river to sleep the day away before heading for Sydney, six hours fast with a dozen cans of beer and the roadside cafes tense and moving oases of ordinariness in the rich night of driving and drinking, speeding and living.

In those early Sydney years Joey had kept away from Robert, his businessman brother — older, respectable, powerful, one of the bosses, married with kids and a beautiful wife who cooked and sewed and shopped and drove the children to school and had ladies in to lunch on the patio. Joey wanted to make his own scene. He moved in a different world, out there, in the suburbs. A man in the boot of a burned-out car, another bloke blasted in his red Mercedes, a body or two in the harbour, off The Gap. Some bird making a fuss taken out into the bush down on the Hawkesbury. Collecting the money from the cafe in Concord, taking a cappuccino with the bagman, walking out into the wonderful blue day, going to collect Lily from Darlinghurst and heading out of town for a few days of fishing the estuaries and eating fish platters for two, huge meals of salt and vinegar and beer in the local RSL Club each night. Lily dressed in her neat slacks and blouse, a cardigan thrown over her shoulders with that style he loved, her hair freshly done, her skin turning pale pink and then lightly freckled in the clear sea air. Living.

3. THE LAST TIME I SAW MY FAMILY

How to explain. It sounds far-fetched and yet it must be a common story and entirely ordinary.

A ruthless man, ambitious, talented, organised, a risk-taker with a superb line in public and private relations. He had a special knowledge, that edge of power and danger, more than bravado. He couldn't meet someone for the first time without drawing them into his circle. He was confident of his grand gaudy world. He assumed all would admire and want to be part of it and he was rarely wrong.

Racing was one of his minor interests played to look like it was all he did. There's a lot of business done on the track, just like there's a lot of business done in the pub, in the office, in back rooms and in meetings in fine rooms across the street from Treasury.

My father was born Fiodor Stanslacht, Frank Smith to the modern society. My mother was Lulu Sidebottom, relieved, I suspect, to be able to change her signature on cheques.

And there were my two brothers, Leon and Arch, and various protégés who took on the name and the business. Smith and Sons, import–export, commissioning agents, investors, company directors.

Arch was the youngest and a manager of several concerns. He had a company car, went on interstate trips, represented the father at the lower or outlying reaches. He was good with people, my father said, a real charmer, and genuine. We all liked him.

Leon was an accountant. His wife, one of the true gems of the world, had come from a trucking family and set up her own car sales business. Straight. Absolutely. And she was good. It was her white Jaguars that took us to the ball where I was a debutante.

SLIDE:

Here is a photograph of Frances Smith at a Melbourne society ball. Season 1966. Partner, film-star-handsome William, son of a white goods manufacturer-cum-head of an agricultural conglomerate, a fine but disinterested pair. I had eyes only for Giorgio, a Greek god who thought I was sleazy, which I probably was, and he in turn lusted after Dame Mary Marmaduke's only child, Annabelle, an angel in off-white lace that showed far too much of her ample bosom. My parents proud. My brothers and their wives terribly handsome in their fabulous evening wear. We all danced all night and felt grand about each other, even mother, still frail after the first attempt at dying gracefully and soon to succeed, though not exactly by her own hand.

My mother must have had it then, holding on, denial, holding it in. She was dead within a month of this photograph and I was gone within a week of that, without regrets.

It was, when I remember it, which isn't often, a very fine childhood. Great parties, family affairs, always lots of people coming out for the weekend or overnight. We had one of the first swimming pools. I rode in gymkhanas, learned to jump. Mother was kind and charming, a really good hostess my father always said. The

57

boys were groomed for the business and never wanted anything else. Why would they?

We moved into town suddenly, or that's how it seemed to me. Dad sold off the stables to his friend and we took over uncle Hebdidge's house in Beaumaris and there were people coming around all hours of the day and night and mother was suddenly taken ill and then a week or two in hospital and dying. It was like a script that had been going on for years without me knowing. I was still in school, sixth form. I went to the funeral and came home and collected my things and left. I haven't seen any of them since that day.

What was it? Horses, rigged races, big bets, big wins, favours, refrigerated trucks, warehouses of electronics and mother making sandwiches for twenty with a laugh and her hair as neat as a magazine photo and the boys wearing suits when they turned thirteen and mum and dad dancing in the big lounge room one summer night and the brothers and cousins and wives standing in a circle and clapping them.

That Christmas we moved into town and the party started and never seemed to stop and mother came downstairs to find the girl blue in the back toilet and she wept for days with anger at her own stupidity.

'Where did you think this all came from?' he shouted.

'Not drugs,' she said, 'not prostitution.'

And in weeks she was dead. I always thought she died of horror, or heartbreak — of a heart broken by her complicity. It was one of those quick diseases, cancer I suppose. It can do that — attack the depressed and unhappy. Self-inflicted death. I left, got a job in town, lived in a rooming house on Puckle Street, went to tech, learnt photography. It was that sort of time — we could be anything and so I was. No past. No worries.

Anne Stevens always wanted there to be a deep end. She probably knew the bones of the story. Her father was the local cop. My father probably paid him off for this and that. She never refers to it although between us there is always an opposition, like we come from two different classes in Victorian England and despite long years of friendship, there is always a point at which we disagree. Today it is on the point of the story.

'What about love,' she says, 'or guilt?' She reckoned I was blocked by some unnameable childhood horror. Her taste for melodrama was wearing, and there were things I didn't tell her. A long love affair that didn't end, just became geographically difficult. Letters across the ocean might sound romantic but after years you forget how to speak the same language.

'Love conquers all,' she would say. 'Love is a by-product of living,' I would reply. There was something very attractive about being alone, enigmatic, almost heroic. Vera maintained it was unhealthy and wanted to talk to me about vibrators and the American way of onanism currently being celebrated in academic circles. She was pleased to hear I went horse riding in Centennial Park, worked out at the Broadway Gym and had a healthy weakness for chocolate.

When I first met Anne's friend Solange she, Anne, had no idea that the apparently mythical lover of letter-writing fame, soul mate and life partner, had been a woman. Solange took a while too, I might add.

4. JOE SIMMS HAD A GOOD DEATH

My reluctance to talk about the past leaves me when I am talking to Harry one night at Le Bar. Anne Stevens is working late and is later still for her date with Harry. He is flagging with exhaustion and the sort of boredom that can hit you when you are surrounded by lots of people having a determinedly good time and you are waiting. Harry is waiting for Anne and I am waiting for the rumoured appearance of Tina Turner. We know each other vaguely and wait together, the fan and the best friend's boyfriend. I'm not bored, I'm excited by these by-the-way times of a big city and the luck, someone real to talk to.

Harry is drinking whisky and so I ask, 'What's the great tragedy today, lost your best friend or something?' He looks at me like I'm a ghost or a cop or worse, a fool. I say, 'I've seen most things in my time. I think we met once in Melbourne. I was just a kid sister, Leon and Arch Smith's kid sister. You came to the house, bursting with excitement as I remember. My father was furious for some reason and Arch was shipped off to Queensland the next day.'

'Yeah. And I did his time for a series of armed robs. I was just a kid myself.'

I grimace disbelief.

'I was driving. Your magnanimous father failed to deliver on that occasion. There were a few like me in Pentridge at the time, quite a club of Smith family fall guys, including the ones who did the cars for that businessman heist that went badly wrong. As I remember, the bastard suffocated in the boot of his own BMW. Stick to Holdens was the word inside, they've got plenty of breeze.'

'And have you?' I ask, uncomfortable with this reference to the lists of the dead.

'No. I got into the muscle game after that, bodyguard, bouncer, number two man on hire to visiting businessmen. It didn't pay as well but it was indoors and safer. Most of the time.'

'Most of the time?' I say, prodding him along with upward inflections.

'I heard a rumour today I didn't like much. Nice piece of work but there'll be repercussions, ripples, bloody shock waves if what I heard is right.'

I wait.

'They reckon they gave him a good time, a real send off. Got some boat down on Pittwater, beer, champagne, lobsters and prawns on ice, real slap-up do, girls dancing in the lounge and four or five blokes laying about, drinking and telling dirty stories and having a great time.

'This bloke is nice and pissed and mellow as hell and starting to reminisce about when he first came to work in Sydney and cracking the big time and making a few real big hits and how he was scared as all shit but got over it. Like play-acting, he said, like getting all the right props and the timing exactly right and always using a different gun or doing a serious bashing with brass knuckles and special boots. When he's all loose and supple and really feeling good they bring out the Smith and Wesson, his own, and he stares at it and at them, face by face, and says: "Hey fellas . . ."

'And they say, or one of them says, "Joey", and he begs and they let him and then they open another bottle of champagne and pour four glasses, leaving his empty, and then they haul him up onto the deck and tie a couple of handy car engines to his legs and push his head over the side and throw a bag over it and say adios amigo and pull the trigger and heave his legs over. His body falls forward and down, going with the force of the gunshot to the head, blood and flesh splatter on the water, down he goes. A real good death.'

The waitress puts another double scotch down on the table and I ask for the same. We might as well get blind together 'cause I certainly don't want to know that I know who the guy was or how Harry got to know so much poetic detail about the scene.

I say, 'I've seen worse,' and 'I guess they had their reasons,' and 'Do you think Tina's gonna turn up, does she like to stay out late?'

He looks at me and laughs with relief. 'You don't care,' he says, almost disbelieving that his story has failed to move me.

'No,' I say, 'I don't. Kitchens and heat. Fire and burns. I'd probably like it better if you told me he bobbed to the surface and suffered for an hour or two, his life crawling slowly before his eyes, his half-a-head aching with an unspeakable pain and his legs being wrenched from his body by sharks and the car engines tied to his feet.' I'm leaning towards drunk as I say this and am immediately sorry. The things you don't know you think until they come out of your mouth.

'You read too much Robert Ludlum,' he says.

I say, 'I never read books. Did they fuck the girls before or after?'

Silence. Not even a look. Going too far. I say, 'I think we'd better have another,' and he tips his empty glass towards me in agreement. Then I say, 'But I really want to know, is it the death that makes them want the sex or the sex that makes them lust for death?'

Tina comes in a little while after and I move up to take some shots. Harry's gone when I look for him and Stevens never turned up. I cut back to soda water and saunter out into the street at dawn. It's a good feeling, a loaded camera, star-gazing, being in the city like this.

I feel like hell next day but it's only the photographic library shift for me and we have a reputation, well deserved, of being grouchy and patronising. I drink coffee continuously and go home to my house in Redfern feeling a little like a very unpleasant sort of death myself and I spare a thought for Joey Simms and his fabulous scenic waterway grave. I think: he lived too long.

5. WHO IS VERA?

Last night with Harry, in Le Bar, I went in fast and looking around, pretending to be a regular. I could tell you an excuse — that alcohol turns me sour — but I'm an enjoyable drunk. I laugh at everyone's jokes. I always go on to the next bar and when the walls shift and move I climb into a cab very quietly and cruise on home. I don't drink for oblivion, I don't drink alone and I never drink cask wine. Underneath all the manic work and forgetting there's a protestant soul that stares back at excess and damage and says no.

I am not a unified subject, I don't think of myself as a whole, and when I listen to Harry's stories and feel the reluctance leave me, slip away, through no desire or action of my own, when I feel like I am toppling, falling over and over, I know I have to put out a hand and stop myself.

When I don't like myself much, when I listen to what I say and hear it pornographic, I call 'home': the utopian not the mythical home. I call Vera McKee, Karella housewife and community worker. She's lived in the area all her life. The salt of the earth. I do not know how she does it. She answers the phone, listens for a minute of two, breaks into my rave and tells me every little thing about everyone from there I do and don't know. Who's died and divorced, had accidents, got killed, gone bankrupt, become a star. It's all there in her small world, plus the kids and the job and Danny, who collects vehicles and machinery and petty offences on his lengthening record.

I am always transported, entranced, taken out of myself and grounded. I always promise to pay a visit soon and never quite get around to it. Or I arrive without notice and stay for a week and sleep like a zombie and leave again, restored, no explanations.

Tonight I ring Vera and I tell her about Joey Simms. 'Yes?' she says, as if that is only the beginning of the story. Then she says, quietly, in her best weary-with-the-pathetic-importance-of-the-urban-world voice, 'Sydney's just another town, Fran, it's just another small town like all the rest in this small-town country.'

She starts to tell me about our old headmaster whose daughter became a junkie and ended up in the bin over at Staunton and everyone knew and the poor man just cracked up.

'Good,' I cut in on her, 'he did more than his fair share of damage to fine minds.' There I go again.

I ask her, just by way of changing the subject and my vicious frame of mind, if she remembers the Newman–Green murders. 'What's the local word on them?' I say. 'You always hear everything.'

There's a long silence on the phone. When she talks again she sounds a long way away. 'It used to be that some local bloke did it and the good men of the town just couldn't believe it, so nothing happened. Then there was the story that it was one of the good men themselves, but that didn't get much of a run. The last thing I heard was that the cops knew who it was and couldn't get enough evidence and now he's left the area and good riddance. Why do you ask?'

It *was* just something to talk about but with Vera there's always got to be a good reason, a really fine reason, a reason that mirrors the power and importance our lives must have if we are to live on this lousy planet at this lousy time and know so much without being able to do anything about it. She's an unapologetically unreconstructed seventies activist and no cynical sleaze-bag artist friend from the city is going to make polite chit chat on her time.

I tell her about meeting up with Anne Stevens and our talks about the past. She says there's always a reason for these things, meetings, conversation, researching and repositioning the world. Vera is doing a post-grad-by-correspondence psychology course and I can almost hear the physical effort that goes into the lines. 'Yeah, Vera,' I say, 'I know all that and Stevens knows it all inside out. I just thought there might have been some news on the case, you know. Her father did it rough over all that and had a nervous breakdown. I guess she's fixated.'

'That Joey Simms,' Vera comes right round the circle, 'wasn't he one of your father's favourites for a while?'

'A long time ago, Vera. That's not why I raised it. Dad's in the clear. He's always in the clear.'

Then she surprises me. 'I saw your father a few months back.' I am silent. 'He was having lunch in the big new Bistro attached to the Outrider Hotel. A big table of men to welcome the old man of the family that owns the place, he's back from gaol. I told you about that, didn't I? How they burnt down the hotel for the insurance money and let the old grandfather do the time because he had less to lose and would get a better deal in Pentridge. Anyway, he's out now and your father was at the lunch.' More silence.

'We said hello to each other and in a very formal and amused way he walked me out to the car park and we stood and talked about the weather and where I was living now. I admired his new chauffeur. She was making calls on the car phone and didn't stop to be introduced. He looked well, fit and happy. We shook hands at the end. I'm a respected member of the middle rank of the community. You know what it's like out here, in a place like this where everyone knows when you sneeze, people like that depend on us to keep the appearances straight. I enjoyed seeing him. He didn't mention you.'

'OK, Vera, OK, I'm sorry I always ring you when I'm in a state but thanks for being there. Thanks.'

I didn't say goodbye or see ya. She'd cut to the bone and I was brim full of hurt and guilt. You shouldn't treat your friends like poker machines. OK. OK.

CHAPTER 5

Anne Stevens has had her hair set. She is wearing a mauve drape wool blouse and a single string of pearls. Her secretary, Deidre, is standing at her right shoulder, leaning over the desk. They are pretending to work on a sheaf of papers. I take the photograph after seventeen attempts to hold the pose — the phones ring, someone pops their head in the door with the latest dingo joke, the phone rings again, we have coffee to discuss the dynamics of the pose, the phone rings three times while we sip and make half sentences. Finally I take the phone off the hook and order them to smile, take the shots and leave, muttering, 'You shouldn't treat your friends like poker machines.'

1. LOOK MAX

When a woman called Louise Andrews telephones for an appointment to discuss a delicate situation requiring the utmost financial and legal discretion, I almost leap down the phone with joy. Here is something, the accent, the soft urgent voice. The word discretion has always been a favourite of mine. She says she doesn't have a problem, yet. She has a feeling. A fear. I suggest she come in at eleven.

I send Deidre off to re-schedule appointments. She can't get onto Max so I steel myself to deal with him quickly. The photographic session hadn't gone as I would have liked. Frances was jumpy, impatient, we grated at each other's versions of ourselves — never work with your friends. Our manners lapse, too much intimacy. I look forward to the distance. She will send the proof sheets and I will choose the frames to be printed, mounted and framed, one for my desk, one for my father. This is how I want to look at myself, calm, professional, woman. I look forward to paying whatever she asks without dispute.

Max is on time and in a talkative mood. The case starts on the following Monday. The judge won't take another adjournment. Max is anticipating the spotlight and for a moment he seems to be about to enjoy it. We become boys at the football club, pumping up for the big game, raring to be out there and at 'em. He paces my expansive office with its million-dollar view and adjusts his eloquence to the surroundings.

'Jeez I can't wait to see those guys squirm in the witness box. You've really got them sweating. We'll be a great pair. I want you to be very serious and a bit humble. Judges like that and it gives the prosecutor a false sense of security. And I'll be making a big effort to be very respectable and hurt, a bit . . . shall we say, wounded, by these terrible allegations. And then you'll hit them with the priors and the self-confessed liars stuff and I'll shake my head and look . . . baleful, yes, balefully at the creep. Not an ounce of threat, I've got to be . . .'

'Mr Cavanagh.' I have to stem the flow of bullshit although I am enjoying the performance. 'It won't be like that at all. You know it. This is the first day. All that stuff comes later and we might never get to that, *if* we play our cards right. Now, I've got another appointment. You'll have to go.'

He's not happy about this. I can see the muscles in his neck clench and relax, his hands come up and he makes himself sit down in the chair opposite me. His hands go on the desk. 'Miss Stevens.' He is trying for the firm but reasonable voice, he fails. 'I'm paying for your time and you'll just listen for a while. This is pretty damn important to me and I'm not having any jumped-up lady in a wig telling me when I can or can't speak. You got that?'

There's no response I can make, no 'Look Max' or 'I know this is hard for you' approach. 'I don't wear a wig, Max, I'm a solicitor, although I'll be appearing for you in court.' There's a silence. I stare back at him, we nod at each other at the same time and I start to smile and he turns away because the look of dread, of fear, of facing the hole he's in, can't be shared. Not for a moment can the weakness show.

'Look Max, let's just take it step by step. You know we can drag these things out for years if we have to. Nothing's going to happen next Monday that both you and I can't deal with. Now, go away and get on with your business. Why don't you set up a few deals, go to the races, act normal? It's not just these guys in gaol who are out to get you. They're working for someone and that someone's out there watching you squirm. Give yourself a few dramatic victories, because there'll be nothing, and I mean nothing, for you to do or say in that court-room. No nodding or looking or play-acting. It doesn't work. The press will tear you apart if you so much as think the judge is a fool. OK?'

He gets up without a word, fists clenching and unclenching. I go with him to the door and shepherd him toward the lift. Louise Andrews has arrived. Deidre is bringing in the coffee. Louise Andrews is chain-smoking and sweating through her silk shirt. Louise Andrews, who doesn't quite have a problem yet,

who has a feeling, a fear. And a lot of special effects
that go towards a story.

2. THE WIFE OF THE EMBEZZLER

Last night Louise Andrews had been awake and thinking, gazing at her reflection in a window turned mirror
by the night. She had cleaned the house all evening,
scrubbed and dusted and put things away, set out the
clean things, doilies, cloths, tea-towels, bath towels.
She had ironed serviettes in neat piles, done two loads
of washing, and hung the clothes out to dry in the
dark. She sat in the big chair, within the smells and
perfumes and odours of Pine-o-cleen, vanilla essence,
Marveer and Mr Sheen, smoking a cigarette, not
drinking. It was eleven p.m. She sat for half an hour
and then went to bed to read three chapters of Anita
Brookner. When she turned the light out and lay awake
in the darkness, her eyes adjusting to the never-dark of
city living, she thought about what she was beginning
to know, inexorably, about her husband, about embezzlement, about how long she had known. The next
morning she woke up and rang a woman lawyer from
the yellow pages.

In my office, coffee and cigarettes send steam and
smoke to the ceiling, the big blue view pours in the
window, she begins to tell me her situation.

'Something has happened, well not happened yet,
although I suppose it has . . .'

She starts again. 'My husband has been embezzling
money for several years, I suppose. I mean, I think I
know that this is what has happened, is happening, and
they're about to close in on him, I think, I mean, I imagine it, I mean, perhaps I am imagining it.' She takes a

deep breath. 'This is what I have come to talk to you about. I think we are about to be found out.'

'How long have you known?' I ask straight off. Then, when she doesn't answer, 'Does he know you know? What does he say?'

'He knows I know something. He won't talk about it. We can't begin to talk about it. I'm in shock.'

Symptoms, remedies, sweet black tea, head between your knees, no that's for fainting. Talk it out, calm down.

'It's this creeping fear. It dawns on you and in a flash you have known forever. We thought we were safe. The distortion of memory. I can't remember when it started, or how we imagined we could just go on. I've become wildly paranoid.'

'That's stupid. You should take vitamin B.'

'I know. Every day I take an early lunch and buy the *Financial Review* and pore over it. If there's a crash coming they will know. There'll be a hint. They can't help showing off. They're a newspaper — breaking stories is their business. We are well-known around town, a good address, designer magazine interiors. There'll be a tip-off. I wait.'

'It doesn't happen like that. Can you tell me what you think he's done?'

'I want to flee, cut and run. I can't stay around to see it all happen. Become implicated. I am implicated. I've been Lee's partner for years, a Company Director, the works.'

'I'm not a specialist in company law. I can only really advise you when something happens. Perhaps —'

'I want practical help, not advice. I've made up my mind, I'm going away. The kids will have to look after themselves.'

'Perhaps you should talk to your husband, get a good business law firm to sort out the books, see exactly — '

'Don't be so stupid. If it was legal, if it was possible to "sort out the books", I wouldn't be here panicking. I kept the books, the real set of books. I'm not a very good book-keeper. Just tell me, what can they do to me? How much time do you get for, say, five million?'

She has stopped chain-smoking, the panic winds down. She's an ordinary-looking woman, a good plain face. She's over-dressed, as is the fashion these days, in some complicated sort of drape suit, skirts over skirts and shirts over shirts. She wears clip-on earrings, an art-work leather belt in three colours with a mother-of-pearl buckle, snakeskin shoes which don't match or tone with anything else. Her head looks too small for all this paraphernalia and I want to tell her to go home and put on jeans and T-shirt and take in the washing and do another round of ironing and scrub all the I'm-sure-they'll-be polished floors and then wax them and shine them and by that time she'll be so exhausted she'll be able to sleep and tomorrow she should have a long talk with her husband and plan what they are going to do.

I tell her to do this, exactly. She looks at me as if I am mad. I am cranky and disappointed. I wanted some nice clean paper case I could get my obsessive teeth into and she blows paranoid smoke signals all around my office. She makes me doubt myself. For a minute there I prefer Max.

SLIDE:

Here is a picture of Anne Stevens coming out of the

court the day Max Cavanagh was found to have no case to answer. Her golden hair is crisply waved and sprayed into place. She wears a black suit and a white shirt, black stockings, flat shoes. She is nearly six foot you know. See, she's standing next to Max, who is just six foot in his shoes with lifts and behind her and to the left is Bryce McLeod, the prosecutor, looking depressed. He's around five six, I guess, and is so dispirited he has already taken off his tie. Max is grinning and I've caught him in mid-step — he looks off balance, leaning toward the camera as if he is both dancing and falling.

PART TWO

A few days

Some days are like the calm ocean gently breaking small waves on pristine beaches. Some days are big seas, storm waves, peak tides, with the Bondi and Malabar outfalls on strike and pumping pure sewage into the sea. See the brown sludge live on TV.

You've got your life set up, it's a late summer going on forever, the beaches are closed and everyone is surprised, shocked, there is outrage. The kids go back to school and the city settles into its perfection — work, sky, seaside, nights of passion and conversation, a certain coherence, order. You spend dangerous time, loquacious, complaisant, content. Coasting. Proceeding. Swimming laps in the salt-water pool, lying beached on the sand in a state of total bliss. The present. That moment when it all makes sense and fits together and you are not at all distressed. Dangerous time.

You shouldn't have said 'It's all right'. You shouldn't have said, 'I'm content.' You shouldn't have said, 'This is what I've always wanted — work, love, friends, conversation.' Days race, you go on doing everything your diary tells you to, things occur, incidents, events, whole worlds change, you want to abandon ship and leap into soft deep sand, pumping the thigh muscles to move.

CHAPTER 6

1. LOUISE ANDREWS REMEMBERS
THE BEGINNING

Lee Andrews looked around at his respectable worried life and could not see anything to know surely. He felt, at times, a great desire to be overwhelmed by the voluptuous prostitute–whore of every boy's imaginings and wept great drops of tears onto the pages before him: bank statements, tax return, cheque book, credit cards, the school fees, the mortgage. There had to be something else. The telephone bill.

He looked up to see the reflection of his wife in the window above his desk. It was late at night. She stood quiet and still as he looked at her. She offered no comfort. She asked no questions of mutual dilemma. He looked down at the cheque butts and bent to the task of reconciliation.

She said, 'Will we manage again this month?'

'We always have.'

They did not start to argue. It had all been said before and they knew it was a battle neither could win and they both hated the predictability, the awful commonness of their struggle with the bills. Like their parents, though they had sworn, promised, believed they would be different. Their plans were careful, knowing, sophisticated, wanting. They always made exact allocations for entertainment and clothes and squandered on new restaurants and silk underwear.

They loved each other's inability to be mean, to be poor. 'We should be sensible I suppose, but it's oh so dreary,' and then they would laugh in each other's faces and sit over brandy as the restaurant emptied and

their desire for each other smouldered, 'like cats waiting for sundown'.

She said, 'Let's go down to the beach, like we used
to, and lie on the grass and be wild.'

Down by the water they sat in the parked car and
worried at the other parked cars up the end of the
clearing and away from the light. 'Kids,' she said. 'We
used to come here. Let's walk, at least along the sand.'
But the wild moment had gone and they sat in their
silence and listened to the waves break, breathing the
thick salty air of the still night. The trees in the park
behind the beach were dark and waiting for the breeze
to come. The light from the streetlight turned Lee's
complexion yellow. Louise sat on the dark side, pale.

'I wish we had some more brandy,' she said, as a car
door slammed at the end of the park and they turned to
see no-one and nothing and went still with instinctual
fear, a tremor, someone walking over graves. What was
it, apart from the children left alone at home, apart
from the speedy emptiness of their finances, apart from
the silence between them that might have harboured
secrets and fantasies or angers or understandings,
speech, that made them look again, a pale arm in a
distant car, a limb contorting perhaps in the actions of
lovemaking, the palm of a hand sliding down a window, like a long slow wave goodbye?

It was in the evening papers. A drug dealer had been
shot at Nielsen Park. A car had been found burnt out.
Burning. The police were asking for anyone with any
information to contact a telephone number. She rang,
anonymously, to say exactly what she had seen: two
cars. And heard: the sound of a door slam. The wave of
the hand. And the time: twelve-fifteen a.m, because we
left straight after and were home by twelve-thirty, and

we live on, at, in, Paddington. From a phone box, not wanting to get involved.

2. ANNE STEVENS AND FRANCES SMITH HAVE DINNER

I could always tell when Anne Stevens was in love, she sang loud choruses from her favourite song:

Your sweet and shining eyes
are like the stars above Laredo
Like meat and potato
to me

In my sweet dreams we are
in a bar and it's your birthday
and we're having a conversation
with Fernando.

'Yes,' I say, 'I can see the simple melody has some heart to it. Trying . . . '

She says, 'It's the break in the voice, and the banality of the things you think about the lover. The perfect lyric is hard to find.'

She is singing the meat and potatoes song in the shower. I am deep in inventing recipes in the kitchen. The telephone rings and I let the answer-phone take it. Cooking is an art and a science and I am a dabbler, creative, successful, consummate. I splash wine into the leeks, peel potatoes precisely, race out for butter in the margarine household and when I get back she is sitting, clean and refreshed and utterly dejected, eating the peas raw and inviting my castigation.

'There were no calls for me,' she says, by way of a half-hearted explanation. I save the peas from early ingestion as she monologues: 'Harry Bean has been around in the distance for so long I'd finally come to believe in his existence.' She pours the cooking wine. I let her. Self-indulgence is necessary but not to be pandered to. She chokes on the rough vinegary white and splutters, 'It's always a mistake to relax,' and 'Men are like cats, you can love them over and over again and they go on walking away with your heart in their mouths. He was so nice.'

'Nice is hardly a heartfelt passion,' I say as I remove the cooking wine to the pantry and open the good bottle. I set the table and turn on some music. I put the food out and we eat in silence, fuelling up. I clear the table and wipe down the kitchen and place the photographs on the table in front of her. I take a notebook from my bag and search for the right pen. I say, 'Work.' Stevens gives up her rending heart and takes the files out of her briefcase. She says dates and names and I write them down.

Here is a photo of Robert, Joe, Lily, Max, with Harry lurking in the background. They are getting off the boat. Here is a photo of Robert with the businessmen, the politicians. Here is Lily outside the mortuary where the coronial inquiry into the murder of her bodiless husband is taking place. In the background, senior New South Wales police detectives in plain clothes are studiously looking elsewhere.

Here is a photo of Robert and Max at a weekend meeting held out in Dubbo in the early 1980s. This photo comes from the collection of one Tim Redonto, now deceased, who was a witness at a Royal Commission and later granted indemnity to speak in the early days of the National Crime Authority. He knew a lot of gossip, gave evidence on several alleged slayings.

It was he who told the story of the young man and the young woman, drug couriers, addicts. She was very beautiful, Annabelle, and he was William. Here is a photograph of them at their wedding. They are excited and scared, you can see that in their eyes. Their life must have been entirely like that. They were twenty-one and twenty-two respectively when they died.

Here is a photograph of Lance Doyle and Drummer Sinclair, taken on a yacht off the coast of New Zealand not too many years ago. Lance is getting fat, starting to blow up like a bloated cow on rich pasture. His eyes are getting smaller in his ballooning face, jowls, he wears a singlet that is stretched over his stomach. He says, I like the good things of life, food and wine.

Drummer (Tim) Sinclair is still pushing himself past his name, his heritage and the fact that his head is too small for his body — even with all that hair and the earrings. His body, too, is thickening and he is not happy about it. He looks at Lance with awe and repulsion, trapped as he is in a business that has only two ends, kill or be killed.

The money's there for the taking if he kills Doyle. Tip the body over the side on the high seas, put the crew off in Nauru and leave them to find their own way back to Europe and take the boat heroically into Coffs Harbour single-handed. Drop the drugs over the side tied to a navigation buoy a mile out. He's laughing in this photograph. The senior Sydney detectives are taking him in from the yacht for questioning and he is laughing with one of them. Perhaps he is telling them about Doyle or Annabelle or William, and the hand on his back is not restraining but congratulating.

We do the photographs, matching them across the years, faces to names. I produce copies, we cut them up. By the end of the evening we have a pretty chaotic chart and a list of questions.

3. JUST WHEN YOU THINK YOU'VE GOT SOMETHING WORKED OUT

I phone Harry Bean at his mother's place, leave a message, wait, put a load of washing on, vacuum the lounge room. I turn the radio on for the news headlines. There it is. 'Max Cavanagh, well-known Sydney underworld figure, was arrested tonight in his Dover Heights home for the murder of Joey Simms. The police statement said . . .'

Harry Bean arrives just after I have finally fallen asleep. I wake to the sound of a car in the street, a door slams, footsteps on the gravel, I go down to open the door. I feel like melting and he strides in and paces my perfectly polished floors and takes swigs of whisky from the bottle. Shouting. I can't be bothered with this. I go back to bed and fall immediately into a deep sleep.

Harry is still there in the morning, snoring on the couch and waking to the smell of coffee. I push him into the bathroom and go out into the bright sunshine of Friday morning, water the garden, sweep the paving, more coffee, bacon and eggs for two on the patio. I am furious with the banality of it all. I don't want a wifely life like this. I go down the street and buy six packets of cigarettes.

I say, 'Let's go down for a swim. It's a fabulous morning.'

He looks at me as if I'm mad. It is six o'clock but he trudges after me and sprawls on the sand sweating and loosening up in the splendid heat of insistent summer. I swim off the small beach. Yes it is cold and yes I do it to show him up. I breast-stroke to the end and turn and come back; that's quite enough for a show off. I come out feeling like Dawn Fraser, flexing my chest muscles and shoulders, breathing deeply before lighting a cigarette. 'What's your problem, mate? This enigmatic silence is not my scene.'

He blinks in the sunlight and I hand him my sunglasses, hating myself. Wifely gestures grate across my soul like Mary Leunig cartoons of women with their hands in the blender.

'OK,' I say, 'life's a bitch but this weather's pretty sweet. Why don't you go for a swim? You'll feel better.'

He does and he does. I resist saying I told you so. It's easy. I was never meant to be a wife. I say, 'OK, you're the man of my dreams and I love you a bit but I'm not going to put up with this strong silent stuff. I've got to get to work. You've got half an hour. What's the story?'

'I saw your mate's name in the paper.'

'It happens sometimes.'

'You're playing with fire. You don't know what you're doing.'

'Maybe,' but slowly, drawn out. I need someone to talk to too. 'Tell me,' I say, 'tell me what I should know.'

Harry Bean sits on my old velvet couch with his head in his hands. I bring the coffee, light one of the specially purchased cigarettes, say, 'Harry, warn me off, frighten me, tell me about Cavanagh and the body in the park, the special relationship with the New South Wales police. Tell me something I don't already know.'

And he says, 'Cavanagh's gone. He's a dead man

walking. Times change. There are always the dispensables. Max is last year's model. Redundant.'

He says, 'Someone I used to know a long time ago is doing time in Mulawa. A woman. That should make you sit up and take notice. A goddamn woman set up, three kids in welfare and no-one to stand up for her in court . . .'

'So. What's this got to do with Max?'

And he says, 'Max is a rat.'

And I say, 'Max is being set up. You know that as well as I do. Even the newspapers know that.'

No room for illusions, no flight from the physical. Melancholy. Honesty. Facing things. I'm not a wife to be protected and come home to. He's not a husband to provide. We make love despite the fear around us, because of it I suppose. It's ordinary stuff. I like his touch, his breath across my chest. In the glare of morning we talk close. I can be knocked sideways by passion, the passion of the body not the words. The morning is Friday, the last working day and everything resumes. I go into the office like a lady lawyer attending to her job. Harry phones at five to five. I go home early to be with him. 'Everything is OK,' he said on the phone. When I get there he is gone.

4. LOUISE ANDREWS REMEMBERS THE END

In the early days they had made a go of it, keeping down the strain of young kids and two jobs with the extravagance of consuming and the excitement of living slightly on the edge.

Then the heights had been scaled, Lee and Louise Andrews had made it and the shiny surfaces of glamour and success were being daily tarnished as the press had a field day at their expense. Lee was gone. The sky was falling and Louise Andrews, making appointments with lawyers, going over and over the evidence, the statements, the story she could tell, was winding up tighter and tighter. She wasn't winning hearts and minds with her wild memories of office parties and deals struck in executive elevators as they glided from car park to penthouse and back again. Sixty-four floors is a two-martini journey, more if you stop at the brokers' floor on the way.

5. ANNE STEVENS THINKS
EVERYTHING IS ALL RIGHT

High gloss paint is the reason why I wanted a place of my own. Everywhere I have lived people have matt-painted peach and rose-orange and tobacco and pink pinkpink with grey that eats light and turns your thoughts to dreadful Sunday afternoons after you have slept late and wasted the day and it is raining and you can't get your washing dry and the television is lousy and you haven't done a scrap of work and the new week looms like a mountain in the mist when you're on a cheap-fare-to-Europe aeroplane and hoping, hoping the radar works.

It does but the person sitting next to you is airsick and taking brandy from a flask to calm his stomach and then he's talking loudly to his wife who in your mind becomes the poor wife and you find yourself wishing that the plane would crash and he would not survive when suddenly the plane breaks through the cloud cover grey and you are in the high blue of dreams and desire and you put your seat back and place your new hat over your eyes and let the steady hum of the engines soothe you over the Indian Ocean. And in this way you are going and gone from matt grey.

6. Louise Andrews goes away to decide

Suddenly she was calm like she hadn't been for weeks. Calm that was also exhaustion, gone to the limits of everything. Louise Andrews stood on the rock shelf in the winter sun, the wind blew up from the south and she faced it, into the spray.

Beyond exhaustion of every sense there is calm. This is what junkies never know, she thought, or the glitterati walking now along the rocks in their high-heeled city boots and loudly fashionable clothes. But we all know contempt, and contempt for our selves. Perhaps.

I have left all that behind me. I won't go back. Not to collect things or make arrangements. It's too hard to live through these hours of drama. I will just go. Now. Take the first flight out and be done with it, this present tense life. There's only the future now and the children will have to make the best of it. At least I'm not dead. There's no tragedy or mourning to visit down the years. Just a premature and inconvenient adulthood. We protect them too much anyway. Others will look out for them and enjoy the chance. Responsibility. They'll be all right.

7. Getting ready

I live in this picture postcard world that is worth the hour bus trip into town and the fact that everything in the shops costs half as much again and there's no nightlife apart from the pub and an occasional cafe and the famous fish and chip restaurant which I do go to quite often. I swim and walk and look and listen to the sea and the sound of the ocean crashing through the heads and at night it is quiet and peaceful, it feels safe and I am lulled here into a smugness both Solange and Anthony refuse to embrace. They prefer life in the fast lane and tell me that tonight we are all dressing up and going to the opening of a nightclub in the city. Solange has brought her tuxedo for me to wear and insists, despite my protests and the gorgeous Italian silk frock I have laid carefully between tissue paper and hold up now for them to admire.

'Very matronly.' Solange has particular tastes. Her business card and stationery are illustrated with a tiny figure, an old strainer post with rickrack braid as barbed wire, a postmodern consultant. The gate is peg board. She consults on these sorts of artefacts.

She likes very much the red stretch rubber brassiere I have bought her as a gift but hands it back to me. 'Just for tonight. Wear it under the tux and your mother's string of pearls,' she advises. 'Very hard and soft. You'll get in.'

Anthony is wearing a fabulous brown suit and beige silk shirt with emerald lurex braces and gold socks. 'Subtle,' I say. 'Do you think the doorperson will get the drift?' Solange brings in a sixties gold lurex dress with cowl neckline, gold stockings and shoes and a red velvet — a deep red velvet — coat. 'Fitted like a pair of hands upon a neck for strangulation,' I say, envious of course. She gets to be the girl and I am stuck with the silk revers of her made-in-Hong-Kong-silk-and-wool-mix tuxedo — American-style, with a long coat and an inbuilt swagger.

I pull on a pair of French blue socks and settle for the Swiss brogues that I have recently bought for comfort, black. I pick up my black felt hat to complete the gangster effect and we are off in the powder blue Cadillac, our lips struck with red and our eyes touched desperate with kohl. I'm cold in the car, the wind sweeps my bare midriff and I reckon style is stupid as we whizz down the 'S' bends at Vaucluse and sweep into Darlinghurst. 'The centre of the universe,' Anthony is breathless with anticipation. 'Don't sing,' I say. Anthony likes to boast his baritone and command of tacky Streisand routines of ten years before. Solange and I have been known to do the doo-wops willingly, but times change. 'Let us arrive with an acceptance of the years about us, adulthood, they like that, the serious oldies paying attention to the new. It might get us through the door without too much humiliation. Besides, we look like we've got money. We have got money. That always counts for something, despite our many years.'

8. Louise Andrews arrives at the airport

Louise Andrews arrived at the airport with plenty of time to check in the hire car and the suitcase. To gate five for seat allocation and then ten minutes before boarding, which was time enough for a beer or a browse in the newsagents for a thick Hollywood gossip tome that promised and delivered flamboyant sex and desperation, suntans and champagne and those lives where there is plenty of money, work is a pleasure and intrigue, betrayal, lust, and true love triumph. She almost bought herself a bunch of flowers. The thought crossed her mind. She didn't have an inkling of the eyes that watched her, the uniformed persons who signalled and nodded and closed in around her. When she presented the ticket for boarding she was asked to come this way please madam and they walked her, one on each side, down the long indoor runway of light and into the blare of TV cameras that had been held off until just the right moment.

It was spectacular. Hot white TV lights and armies of media, police, airport security and the general public uttering instructions and opinions to each other in raised voices. A single policewoman stood resolute at her side throughout. Louise Andrews had not imagined this.

It had happened quickly, they had kept her moving and she had been told nothing. She stood surrounded by officials and police. Superiors of different services consulted each other and made on-the-spot decisions as the crowd gathered and gawked and asked each other what was going on. The newspaper, radio and television people crushed together for their own dramatic effect. They could not speak unless they were shouting and it was ten to five and they might just have time to rush footage direct to air if the inspector in charge and the airport importants could agree on the appropriate wording.

The crowd muttered and announced, it was someone famous, Elton John, a visiting head of State. Louise Andrews didn't look like any of these people but these days you can't really tell, middle-aged women could just as likely be visiting controversial professors or drug couriers, and the media presence could just as easily be the work of a good publicist. Perhaps it was Spike Milligan's mum or a relative of royalty leaving her husband for a pop star.

Louise Andrews looked directly at the policewoman at her side, waiting for her to speak.

'You are being arrested as an accomplice to fraud. Your husband will be in custody about now,' she looked at her watch. 'I'm Constable Miller. You'll be taken to the airport security suite and from there to Central police cells.'

Louise Andrews looked at her own watch, 5.06, it was digital. Perhaps this slight detail was her downfall. A lapse of taste. Constable Miller nodded to someone in a business suit across the room. The wife of the embezzler was led off past the police inspector making a statement for the news programmes. 'Five million dollars . . . major police operation over several months . . . successful conclusion . . . part of our campaign . . . the fight against corruption . . . these people.'

She remained silent. Speechless. No banal first sentence would fit this cast-of-thousands scene. She had not imagined this.

She had enjoyed making the false trail. A passport, a domestic flight from Sydney to Adelaide in another name, another flight in another name from Adelaide to Perth, then a ticket to Amsterdam in her mother's maiden name to be collected at the Perth Hilton. A stash of English ten pound notes and the numbers and credentials for the bank accounts in Spain and Switzerland. Safe as money in the bank, she had giggled, drawing up the list of names and tickets and departures and arrivals, stopovers in strange cities, sights to be seen, telephone calls to make, those letters of explanation to write and send. She was planning on Scotland eventually. It would be going on to summer there and she imagined long nights of sunshine and climbing mountains in the mist, nothing beyond that.

There comes a time when criminals forget their chosen status and behave as innocents, as ordinary people with predictable daily lives. This might have been the wife of the embezzler's mistake. A failure of the imagination and realising that, beyond a certain point, it is normality that is the myth.

Behind the door off the corridor Louise Andrews was directed to a chair, told that she was formally arrested, a little provincial ceremony, the requisite words and no pomp or drama. There was talk of handcuffs. She remained silent. She leaned forward with her elbows on her knees, staring at the floor, listening to the normal voices around her. She was trying to maintain that even breathing they say can control panic. The Inspector barked at her and she started upright with fright, the first sentence formed: 'Can I have a cigarette?'

9. GOING TO THE NIGHTCLUB

We arrived at exactly the right time. A queue stretched to the corner and people hovered on the opposite footpath to see what was going down tonight. We 'went down' of course. Solange and Anthony knew the owners or the bouncers or someone and we glided up the staircase to the grand entrance hall — red carpet and marbled stairways going in all directions. Figures stood around in serious conversation, not looking at the new arrivals who entered. The music sound was faint. The boom boom of the bass and the incessant percussion was muffled by the thick matt paint pink on orange on peach walls that made me sure that grey would loom up soon.

It did: grey on grey on grey in the main room; silver ceiling, but somehow tasteful; several mirror balls of varying sizes twirling and throwing the light; thick grey carpet, the colour of the Prime Minister's hair, which gave way to a slate dance floor covered in twenty layers of estapol. It gleamed and bounced the sound of a thousand rubber-soled crash step athletic fabulous dancers working up a sweat in their carefully dishevelled clothes, petticoats and black fit tops. White white shirts and loose dark trousers for the boys, red lipstick, or blue, tonight. Red eye shadow like new brutalities loomed out of the noise and said, 'Hi darling, so glad you could make it. It's really sweet tonight.' Anthony disappeared immediately 'to check out the drugs'. He came back an hour later with a friend and a line of cocaine and we went off to the ladies toilets and returned to the pulsating room and danced with strangers and stayed doing that sort of thing for hours.

10. Louise Andrews is charged

At Central Police Station, forms filled, fingerprints — very slow and downbeat compared to the airport scene. They had gone through her bag and given her the cigarettes and lighter and she sat now in a half cage (was she half dangerous?) and smoked and wished she had something to read. Through the long night she moved along the bench as other suspects came and went.

11. At the club

It was four in the morning. The crowd had peaked and ebbed. I had seen a hundred faces I knew and been introduced to a hundred more. I had seventeen new friends and this guy was buying drinks for the room. Just got out of gaol he said, looking like a Paris fashion designer with his sprung body and superb suit, his hair greying at the temples and his hands as steady as rocks. I leaned towards him, 'What do you do,' I said, 'when you're not in gaol?'

'I shoot people,' he said, 'or not, as the case may be. I've got a lot of interests, things going, deals in the air. I make money and take risks, you know, a regular businessman and I can tell you,' he said, leaning towards me but speaking for his own pleasure, 'I like all this new talk of deregulation, the free market. Crime's always been *laissez faire*.'

I say, 'I don't believe you, and, even if I did, I'm not impressed.' He doesn't hear me. I say, 'The level playing field, user pays and what's the market price for a hit these days?'

'Fifty, one hundred and two hundred thousand,' he says, a pause, 'depending on who. That's everything. Absolutely secure. No risk. Like the Winchester thing.'

I had to admire that. 'It's a buyer's market.'

I walk away. Nightclub patter. I'm a maniac-magnet. The whole night is like that, deals and money, playing one city or another. Solange is talking the club owner into an immediate refit. 'The grey on grey on grey,' she says, 'it's old London. In New York white is a statement, real colour, that's where the future is.'

12. FRANCES AND SOLANGE

Solange is as striking as a match. Solange who calls herself Irmgard Louella Persephone Isobelle, or May Agnes Gertrude, is stunning, someone entirely surface, an image, a series of images. I reach for the camera and start shooting. She turns to look straight into the lens, looks away, resumes her casual self.

Seduced by the image in the frame, the light on her

skin, off her skin, the eyes, always looking at something, never looking at herself. Something different, a painting or sculpture come to life and no clicks, snaps, whirrs, or flashes, interrupt the flow. And when she is still, there is the same sense of movement. She is both perfectly plain and a languid assured beauty.

I've been to Rome. I've been to Paris. I've seen the bones. I've captured the lines and the light, just right, on the roof tops at dusk, pink, and cream, like an Impressionist painting. She is the lady in the white dress with black dots in the garden at lunchtime. She is walking away. I am someone out of frame, passing by.

This is one of those high Sydney nights, clear and bright and promising and delivering heat like bathwater on tap. The spray from the ocean seems to go right into the city. Everywhere you can smell the salt, the sea air, the atmosphere of being here. And we are here, in the nightclub of the moment, sweating against the crowd, shouting over the music, turning away, to the next conversation, part of the room. I move on. I'm supposed to be shooting the crowd for the new music magazine that is trying to capture the burgeoning club scene, shooting stars, flames leaping in the firmament of art and culture. I get paid a hundred bucks and don't have to dress for the door.

I drift off into a lounge where the really cool people are semi-prostrate with their leather coats flung within arm's reach and there are jeans to be seen. I have to shoot in black and white but I load a colour film for these cool deal-makers, theatre people, comedians and computer hackers. I take sweet romantic frames for the we-want-to-tell-the-world-we-are-in-love couples who anchor groups of friends to quiet tasteful tables while they cruise the next generation for a new idea.

Who knows who they are. I cannot imagine. Simone is taking notes and shepherds me to her subjects. I snap. She matches them all up later. I refuse to take photos of people who pose. This gives them the shits. They do and they don't want to be in the papers. Which paper is it? They are not sure. 'How do you know when you're famous?' Martin asks Tania. They smile at each other. 'You know when you're not,' she says, and they laugh together. Snap. Click. Whizz. Whirr. It adds something to the beat. A certain *frisson*.

I swing the camera up for a shot of two enemies kissing the air, quite near each other's cheeks. They exclaim and grimace, eyes widening and narrowing as they look over each other's shoulders for escape. Anne Stevens watches this fine performance and is laughing at a familiar face in the background, a man watching from a doorway, moving toward her, saying, 'Haven't we met before?' and they lean towards each other. Harry Bean, by design or accident, is in the right place at the the right time.

13. I CHECKED THE ANSWER PHONE WHEN WE CAME IN, SIXTH SENSE

'I missed you,' I say as we go out into the street.

'You missed a lot of things,' he says as we drive towards Watsons Bay and the sunrise.

'Stop right there,' I say. 'I don't want this high crime life in the fast lane line any more. It's not funny and I'm not part of it and if you are I don't want to know one bloody whisper about it. OK?'

We drive in determined silence. I sweep into the house and turn on the answer phone. There are people who want to talk to me, I signal. There sure are. I change from tuxedo to Fletcher Jones while the coffee is brewing and drive back through the dawn to Central Police Station. A few words with the police and then to Louise Andrews. She says yes and no, yes and no, and I say a major criminal charge, bail will be in the tens of thousands. Does she know anyone who can pay that much? She goes silent, racking her brains for anyone she knows in a position to help. She has no sympathy for herself. There are people who will help and people who won't, can't. Easiest would be Ian Johnson — an old and occasional friend who has property. She hasn't spoken to Ian for months, hasn't spoken to anyone for months. Louise lets her mind float. There must be someone — that teacher at the children's school, a likeable chap, soft and earnest and genuinely friendly. She is shocked at her desperation, the unreality of her ideas in this most real moment. Strangers.

14. BACK AT THE CELLS

The police sergeant tells Anne Stevens they will be going to the early morning court. The boys in grey want everything fast and watertight and ready to stand up, every word. This is bigger than a simple fraud. This is anti-corruption action front page. Louise Andrews sinks back at this description of her predicament. This brief hiatus in a police station might be the last moments of calm. They are not going to be easy on her. The dreams are over.

15. THE NIGHT IS OVER

The club crowd is fiamboyant and loud before departure. Parties cluster for a last drink, pose drunkenly for a last photo they find fabulously amusing now but will regret tomorrow when their mothers ring to comment. Photographs of loose faces, slack mouths, sweet smiles turned to horrible grimaces, uncontrollable muscles. The effort is extreme and the expressions are ghastly, grotesque. I take the photos anyway, the sub-editors love them, merciless.

I move easily through the dishevelled scenery, limp limbs, blurred faces. Over there someone is smiling warmly at her friend, who is weeping quietly. The club owner is full of energy and excitement — it's been a great night, a great take. I take his picture, a handsome man, crisp and neat, while all around him fade with the daylight. He turns away from the camera and goes towards the office. He makes the doorway just in time, collapsing on the leather couch within.

I stand in the street with Solange and Anthony. They are walking home to be safe. Anthony is tipsy-tired and Solange is loose and weaving, from the dancing she says, shaking my hand formal and intimate. 'Goodnight my dear, so pleased to have run into you. You've been on my mind. Come to dinner Monday night. You know where I am.'

I knew. Garden flat with water view, downtown Point Piper where the lawns run to the harbour and the private jetty is great for a view of the Opera House on cracker night. I walk up to the main road, light coming into the sky, shift workers on their way. I hail a cab and arrive at work, complete concentration for one more hour, proof sheets, notes for the day shift. I stagger home by eight a.m. and fall into dreamless sleep.

16. BAIL HEARING

The court appearance before a magistrate is brief and clear. The bail figure of $200,000 makes her gasp. 'It must mean that he's got away.' And it does. Stevens gives a run-through of what would happen next, a picture of expectations. 'You'll be in the remand section. They'll give you a shower and a change of clothes, take your photograph. It's not so bad as long as you do what you are told. Try to sleep. I'll call you tomorrow morning and come out early next week.' Out in the corridor Stevens argues with the investigator hovering with questions. They want to take Andrews to the National Companies and Securities Commission offices. Several phone calls get made. Slow, drawling questions. 'What d'ya think of this mate, we bring her down to you for a while and back up here for the D's at lunchtime?' They wait. Everything is so slow. Stevens asks her again about the bail money. She says, 'I don't know anyone. It doesn't matter.' The day proceeds as a series of long waits, theatrical questions, interminable discussions of what to do next. Finally she climbs into the van and is driven through the peak-hour traffic west into the sunset to Mulawa, the women's prison.

17. SATURDAY, AROUND MIDDAY

Anne Stevens arrives at my house in Redfern around midday looking like a ghost and talking in monosyllables. 'Let's drive down the coast,' I say. 'Come on, you need —'

'I need to sleep for a week but I guess a weekend will do. Thanks.'

As we drive south she relaxes. 'Would you mind not

smoking in the car,' I say, 'I've given up again.'

'Fine.' She shrugs and looks out the window at the passing suburbs. 'Where are we?'

We are driving across the high country between Sydney and Wollongong. The bush is low wind-swept scrub and you can see for miles in any direction, sandstone bush, a great deal of sky. The sun gleams on the future. I say this to her and I can feel her giving up the struggle to be depressed.

We come down the scarp at Stanwell Park and the sweep of the coast to Wollongong takes our breath away. We stop to look, standing at the top of the cliff and letting the wind blast our dreadful furrowed faces into exhilaration. We walk along the beaches and rock platforms as far as we can go. The clouds blow up from the south but the sun shines until it goes down early behind the scarp. The ocean way out is a dull silver. On the horizon and through a sun mist, a three-sail yacht passes like a ghost ship and we begin to make up stories — a present, a myth — that pacify the unspoken fears.

We stay overnight in the house on the cliff above the sea. Stevens starts talking the next morning. She tells how she had come back from the bail hearing to find a postcard under her front door, and Harry still asleep inside. Things closing in, too close to deal with, too close to ignore. She places the postcard writing-up on the table between us. I read it:

> Found you babe,
> there's more work for the willing.
> Watch the weekend papers,
> I always make bail. Ring me.
> Max.

She says, 'I've been advising this woman. She was charged last night with fraud and embezzlement. We could have gone to the Commission and sorted things out — the husband was already out of the country. She could have played it dumber and smarter. I believed her bravado. I failed to give her hard advice. I suppose no-one need ever know. Now I am looking at a woman in gaol. Well, yesterday I was looking at her across a laminex table in the interview room at Central. I start to tell her what's going to happen. She stops me and says she will plead guilty, the husband is gone, offshore like the money, and she gives me the numbers of the bank account in Switzerland. "Bargain with that," she says, "if there's anything left. If the money's gone, sell the house — the title deeds should be in the safe at home — put the children into boarding school. They'll be better off there." As if it's as simple as that. Anne Stevens magician next.' She fakes a laugh. I maintain my nodding silence. What can I say?

18. LOUISE ANDREWS GOES TO GAOL

Going to gaol is not one smooth straight process. There are endless details, phone calls, arrangements. The van might or might not come to pick you up. You might have to spend the weekend in the cells. This is some sort of threat. I remain silent and numb. The van does arrive, right on time, and I climb into it, at least something is happening. Already I feel grateful, servile, tell me what to do and I will do it. I can feel myself going towards the relief of the punishment, at least the tension, the waiting, the not knowing, is over.

There is already a woman in the van. She speaks as I climb in and move along the metal seat. 'Christ,' she says, 'you're one of those suburban types.' She itemises, 'Matching shoes and handbag, both Italian, a throw-over coat, all wool, a silk scarf, Hermes, am I right?' I nod. 'Gotta know the merchandise if you work the stores. Bet ya thought you'd never get caught.' I nod and look suitably embarrassed. 'I'm gonna have to do you a favour or two,' she says, shaking her head and laughing. She is being kind, friendly. I am surprised. 'Thanks,' I say. 'Have you —'

'I been out for a day in court. I get to see me kid. A sister brings him in. Well, she's not *my* sister like, but a sister. You don't know nothing, do you? Got any kids?'

I nod but cannot speak. I realise I don't have to say anything. This large friendly woman knows all about me. I am grateful for the silence. The van stops somewhere and the other side is loaded up, three guys in full voice.

'Just do what I do, OK. Listening, OK?'

I listen. 'Hello darling, how many of ya in there? Two? Great, there's three of us, can you go three between two?' they say.

'Sure honey,' she replies, easily. As easily as she spoke to me.

'Come on come on, what do we do, come on, talk dirty to us, OK? I gotta lot a cock here, dripping for ya, what ya gonna do eh?'

'Anything you like honey, I'm gonna — '

'Suck it eh, ya gotta good mouth eh, big enough eh?'

'Sure sugar and then we'll go somewhere nice and quiet and I'll rub myself — '

'Jesus come on come on we haven't got a lot of time. You had two guys at once before?'

'Yeah it's good — '

'An' what about the other one? Come on honey,

102

don't be shy or are you one of those stuck-up bitches? Don't ya know how to talk dirty? How big's your cunt? Ya gotta good pair, eh?'

She looks at me and nods, fierce and laughing at the same time, and I say 'Yeah, great tits and a cunt just dripping for you . . .'

'What about up the arse mate, oooh, d'ya like it European?'

And I go on, moaning and speaking and she's helping me out and we're both taking this very seriously because the threat comes through the iron wall in the van and I am so pleased they can't see us, and that I can't see them and we drive on into the sunset, we really do, because the women's gaol is out west and it's peak-hour and we talk hot and dirty all the way through the slow peak-hour traffic until we arrive at the gaol and I know nothing could be worse than that and we get to the admissions gate and she pushes in front of me and says, 'This girl's too green, ya gotta put her in a cell block,' and strides off as if she owns the place with a wave goodbye as I go for my shower and search and collect the clean set of nightwear and my own toiletries sealed in plastic and a meal of cold beans and stewed meat and up to the cell block with a view towards the sunset and ten other women just like her and just like me and the long still night, brittle cold air and the lights on outside. I climb into bed and masturbate very quietly.

19. BACK AT THE HOLIDAY HOUSE

The picture on the postcard from Max is a painting: 'Pacifique' by Colville, 1967. I study it, make a list of its elements: blue trousers, sky, sea. Lines of blue-grey, blue-green. Torso, back view, louvres, the louvres frame the wave about to break. A man stands at a window facing the ocean. His back is towards us. He is leaning against the door frame. On the table there is a wristwatch, a gun, a ruler.

Eight blue-grey tones, five frames, smudges of dirt, stains from glasses on the veneer table with the gun and the ruler. A table like the table in the house where we're staying.

She says again, 'I have been representing a woman — she has been charged with fraud, embezzlement, you might read about it in the papers.'

'I never read the papers.'

'She's been arrested. I'll have to go back and see her, organise the defence. She'll get five to ten years.'

Then she says, 'Do you have a gun?'

I say, 'I could get one. Now?'

I go up the back road to Martin's place. He works in the theatre and has a hoard of props and licences, gunpowder, a gun — a Smith and Wesson, from a Mamet play he's been working on. She draws a ruler on the table and places the gun across the ruler. She takes off her shirt and leans against the open doorway, looking out, her back to the room. She says, 'When the sky is very pale and the sea a silver-grey, take the photo.'

I think she is going mad but take the photo. The painting is photo-realist, American, I think.

She says, 'I've done some work for a bloke, he's a crim, up on various charges of conspiracy to murder. He gets off, they charge him with something else. He's been arrested again, for the murder of Joey Simms. There's too much coincidence here.'

'Are you scared of him?'

'No. It's not that. Or, it's not only that. Lily Simms

told me a lot of things all those years ago. I didn't believe much of it. You know what I'm like. Always think
I can see the bullshit. Or could then.'

'Joe Simms' wife, the one who was raped?'

'Twice. The first time was by these guys, thugs,
crims, a pay back — her husband was a hit man. She
told me this guy stood and watched, the boss, Max.
She said that later, years later, when they went back to
Sydney and they were part of the scene, that Max was
there, a friend of Joey's, and she never said a word. I
think about her a lot. I think she was the reason I gave
up being a therapist and took up law. You know, some
mad idea that I could put guys like that away. I defend
them.'

'You could stop. Do something else.' It's a reasonable suggestion. Anne Stevens takes it. Nods. 'Louise
Andrews says the reason why the economy's so bad is
because everyone is corrupt. She gave me this book to
read.'

'I never read books.'

'Listen to this:

But deep down it's anarchy, the unabashed Law of
the Jungle. Hot competition prevails between ascen-
dant States to lock into the volatile hot money market as it races across the globe. Coincidentally, it hits
the south-west Pacific just in time to crash in on
Australian financial deregulation . . .

What are the financial implications of the sub-
stantial heroin trade in Australia? What is the impact of hot money flows on the disastrous escalation
of Sydney property values? A five billion dollar dis-
crepancy (balancing item) exists in the 1988-89
'balance of payments' figures, unofficially attributed

to undetected real estate transactions financed offshore . . .

. . . fragments . . .

. . . the International Monetary Fund 'launders' the dirty processes of a network both elite and criminal into the failures of the nation as a whole, redistributing the burden to the innocent. Latin hot money leads to 'national debt'. Enter the IMF, blaming debt on public enterprise, welfare spending, high wages — all the usual impediments to the free market system . . .

Thousands of . . . highfliers staff public and private bureaucracies retailing idiocies about the financial system. Where is the dividing line between those knowingly on the take and those who are manifestly stupid?'

'Reading books makes you unhappy,' I say. 'You're a lawyer and a reasonably good one. You can't win 'em all.'

'I can't win the right ones,' she says, 'the ones that matter,' slashing at herself with the knives of female guilt.

I take the gun back up the hill road to Martin and we sit and talk into the night about plays and performances and gossip, the unreal world. I take photographs of the lights of Wollongong with a telephoto lens. They might come out interesting. I use a red filter and a yellow filter and slide film. We smoke joints and get silly and I drive terribly slowly down the hill road, creeping around the hairpin bends. Stevens is still up when I arrive at the house. She makes me a cup of tea and says she is going back to town early tomorrow, she'll catch a commuter train in the morning. 'Thanks,' she says, 'I needed to get away.' She leaves at six o'clock while I am still asleep. She takes the postcard and leaves the list. I take a photograph of it.

20. Monday, captured by Max

Train journeys are for thinking, the passivity, that movement forward, cocooned, suburban backyards, that sense of looking out from a position of safety. At Central Station I sat on the orange plastic seats and wished I was waiting for another train. I drank plastic coffee and smoked, watched the crowds ebb and flow and struggle with their luggage and find their friends and feed the pigeons and finally, because I was more frightened of becoming publicly hysterical than anything else, I caught a taxi home.

He came in the door after me, fast, must have been waiting all day. He grabbed me and stuffed something in my mouth, tied my hands and feet and slung me over his shoulder and out the back door and into the boot of a car. A timelessness came over me and my heart slowed to a faint tap and I lay there in the darkness and leaked a few tears of bitterness, stupidity.

I must have slept.

When I come to I am in the boot, the smell of oil and rubber reminds me. The car is still, I can hear traffic in the distance and domestic sounds, radio, television, voices, kitchen sounds, closer.

The boot opens after a while and hands untie my feet and arms, pull me out and upright and reach to take the gag off. Turn my chin, one punch, I guess. Unconsciousness.

There's a radio on in the next room, a television overhead and he says, 'Now we'll talk. No screaming, not that it'd matter round here.' I hear sirens in the distance and think it must be evening as the cool air comes over me like a drug. He's saying, 'Do you want to tell me what you know or will I beat it out of you?'

'What, Max? What do you think I know?'

'Names, Miss Stevens, who came to see you, what did you tell them, who's doing this to me?'

I am tied to a chair at ankles, knees and thighs. My wrists are fixed straight down the chair legs at the back at the wrists. There are good thick ropes around my torso at the elbow. These ropes seem to cross over behind my back and come up over the shoulders and under the armpits. I know what a trussed chook feels like. I take in this elaborate bondage and take a guess at Max's question. 'You think I told someone that you killed Joey Simms?' No answer. I'm on the right track. 'How would I know that, Max?' He comes up close as if to turn my head for another neat punch. I flinch and he slaps the plaster back across my mouth.

21. FRANCES

Deciding to relinquish the pleasure of solitude: all the best romantic images are of the solitary, the alone. I am not romantic. I come up off the beach at the end of the day and taste the salt on my skin. The weather is full of wind and the waves are huge. I watch them for an hour as the light fades and it is time for a glass of wine. I close the curtains and listen to the wind as I put out a solitary meal, one glass. Martin floats in and I take out another plate and another glass. He is in love, he is telling me, I resist a reciprocal revelation. But I am in love in my own way. I take the time to relish the solitude and to organise some of the power. To be seduced, courted, an object of lust, these are pleasures of a different order. I phone Solange and make my apologies, 'I won't be back in town tonight, perhaps tomorrow, if you are free.'

'I am free,' she says, 'for you.' Is it the telephone that encourages these soap opera sentences? Martin leaves before the bottle is finished and I take it out into the wind. The clouds move fast and low across the sky, it is so cold it could snow. I go inside and pile wood on the fire to make a heat wave. It blazes as I sleep. I wake at regular intervals to check, to admire, to anticipate.

22. IN CAPTIVITY

I have never felt attracted to the idea of bondage for sexual pleasure and there is no pleasure, sexual or otherwise, in being tied to a chair and asked questions that cannot, physically or theoretically, be answered. I don't know anything more than a hundred others know with greater accuracy and evidence. I have no intentions. Nothing I say or do can make things worse for Max Cavanagh. I feel light-hearted, as if I could float up in the chair and perhaps drift out the window. I look at Max with detached amusement — three elaborate ropes and cords are definite overkill. My good strong positive thinking shudders and trembles; I am shaking all over and furious.

Max says, 'I saw a friend of yours the other day. I went to see the widow Simms to try and get some information on this frame-up. She knows everyone, used to, and so I went to see her and she says, "I see you've got yourself a lady lawyer. Innocent again?"

'She said she knew you, in another life. I can tell you I didn't like it, too close. She said, "She knows her stuff but what sort of stuff is that to know, Max, between you and me?"'

Fear flattens my fury. It is as if a cord has snapped in my brain and is resounding. My body goes rigid. I feel the insistent pain of the ropes. I hear everything through static.

He continues, 'I think she's having a go at me and then I remember, although I hadn't forgotten. I don't forget a thing. I'd been working for Billy Banister and she was shacked up with Joey Simms and he'd done a job for Teddy Rinblade, you know, that loser from Coogee. When he was carving his name on the eastern suburbs, he had some guy blown out of the water, Tamarama Beach. It was famous for a minute but these things go. I remember it because I swim at Tamarama every day, all year round, and I couldn't that morning. There was blood on the sand and those fluorescent bands up and coppers everywhere. I mean I was clean but what does that matter in this State? You can imagine what they'd have done with Max Cavanagh, "Returning to the scene of the crime."

'Everyone knew it was Joey. He was making his name at the time — take on anything for anyone. Boy did he do some damage, stupid arsehole. You'd never credit he was Robert's brother. Now that's a smart man, real smart.

'Anyway, Joey blows this poor bastard junkie drug dealer all over the beach, real nice stuff, finesse. Reckons he owed Rinblade ten thousand, but the coppers had taken the lot and left the bastard to sweat, same bastards that were "taking statements" from witnesses and talking to the press. Jesus.'

I start to feel sick, real nausea, thick and mobile, coming in waves up through my stomach to my throat.

Max Cavanagh had done ghastly things to people, to people I knew, to Lily Simms. I had heard this story before, told differently. I try to hold the tension in my brain, to close down the body with concentration. I imagine the worst and go into a state of wild thinking that requires total stillness. Nothing to provoke. I keep the vomit down. The sticking-plaster gag is almost a relief. I could not have spoken.

Max is going on, 'Lily reckons Joey was a beautiful man. She says he was set up all along the road. Stupid bastard, I always said, told Robert. He just smiled his cheesy smile and patted me on the arm, "It's all going according to plan." That was his standard line. Never did trust that bastard. A real double-dealer. Anyway, this junkie was Banister's boy and he wanted something done about Rinblade and his thugs and so we went out and beat up the sheila and a few of the boys had a go at her. I called them off. It was regulation behaviour in those days, still is if the truth be told, and she'd worked up the Cross for long enough — wasn't anything new to her I can tell you. Couldn't see the point of it myself but that's the way they like to play it — subtle. Banister said he didn't like blood on the beach either and he liked his dealers alive and paying. In debt, he'd say, is worth ten corpses any day.'

I rock slightly back and forward in my bound state. I set up a rhythm with the sound of his voice going on. I watch his face as if I am paying attention. His skin is pale on face and hands — this man's work is done inside or at night. His face looks pasted on like a mask, like a man who has had a facelift, skin over bones, but thick, a thickening gauntness. I had thought him handsome for a moment in my office that first morning.

'Anyway, Joey Simms gets home and finds his wife

all bruised and battered and Robert calls me in the next day and says, "Max, you got a family, your part of this deal, you —"'

Max has a family? It's never occurred to me before. There was no wife in court, not a mention in the newspapers, nothing in the files, and he says, 'Yeah. Pretty neat eh? I've got three kids, all at university. A wife who cooks and keeps the house just so. I've got a house and two cars and no-one has ever touched any of it. I've kept them safe and well.'

'What's she like?' I wanted to ask. Suddenly it's important to know about this woman and these children, living a cowering life of luxury somewhere with dobermans and electronic alarms and he says 'No. They don't stay safe and clean if I talk. Not even to you Miss Innocence and Accumulation.'

I suspend disbelief for the sake of the play. His play. People like him don't have clean neat safe families. This exclusive boys' club does not admit of wives and families, children in schools, domestic regularity. But of course it is so. People live, eat, breathe, shit. They go about their business as business. And these people more than most. They have ordered, careful lives, aware and watching, moving and calculating, planning and executing. I resettle these images into my brain, this kidnapping is the act of a man on the edge, tipped over, desperate. He's panicked beyond reason. He is talking to me because he's scared he will talk to someone else to save himself. The police. Partners. They would not take kindly to his changing sides, and of course he would have to talk about them. That's a short road to a shallow grave. His panic is real. I cannot argue with him. For once in my life I have to keep my mouth shut and listen. I become perversely grateful for the gag.

Suddenly he stops talking and the silence, my staring and his waiting, terrifies me more than the stories he is carefully telling. I close my eyes and bring the rocking back to the faintest of movements. Sweat runs slowly down my sides. I hear him walk across the room, away from me. I hear him in the shower and this is strangely reassuring. I am conscious of his near-nakedness, the wet towel, the newly-laundered perfume of a tracksuit being pulled on. I smell coffee. I smell whisky. I concentrate on these scenic details as he talks. I smell sweat — my own sweat and it is rancid with fear. He sits back in his chair across the room and goes on.

He is warming to his story, confessing, boasting. I take long deep slow quiet breaths and open my eyes again. I listen very carefully and watch him now with fascination. The sweat dries and I can taste the salt on my lips. He is saying, 'When I went to work for Robert, he was "the man", ran every club and casino, every deal and dance hall worth a buck. Had it all sewn up, landmarks, social pages, even played on the stock exchange, but always, his shares in the black economy were highest. He was the best. I can tell you, I've been working for him for thirty years. I've made promotions, acquired shares, been paid dividends, bonuses, the lot. When Joey went I was like a brother, family he said, trusted.'

He is a long way back, in the past, and I recognise the process, his need to say everything, to speak his story and be heard. I begin to flex my muscles, to work on the numbness that comes with stillness. I twitch my toes, clench my leg muscles, my buttocks, and make tiny movements with my hands. For long minutes I endure pins and needles the length of my limbs, but the blood is moving and I am turning fear

113

into attention, readiness, hope.

'. . . had this place down in William Street, gone now, sold off to a hotel, made a real killing on it I can tell you. Ancient crumbling stuff, a maze of warehouses, offices and clubs. Used to collect a fortune from the dame who ran a place for fags, real class stuff then, leather lounges, discreet rooms, handsome waiters. They came from interstate, Brisbane, Melbourne, and every sort, bankers and cops and school teachers and street boys. Jeez the Americans loved it, every sort of drug and open all night . . . In the daytime it was empty, like a shell, no, like a cave . . .'

Max goes for a piss. The memories excite and console him. It's old times and good times and a past he's lost. I think, a past we've all lost, I hope, and know it's not like that.

He comes back with a mug of real coffee and sits in front of me, sipping, leaving it, waiting for it to cool down. I admire this particular cruelty. I'm tied to the chair and all my senses lean towards the blissful aroma of the coffee. I feel defeated by this small torture, exhausted. The monologue goes on. I don't hear all of it, something about how they decided to get into drugs and all the negotiations involved, meetings, the Americans fading out, getting marketing advice, calling in the consultants, said to go out west, into the suburbs. Plugging into record companies, marketing boyos, hanging out with the growing ranks of the unemployed, school kids' parties and mates, always mates and bastards. Then someone riding in on their hard work and how they sorted it out, had access to the cops, great guys to drink with . . .

I fall asleep. When I come round — from a wild dream of being in London and asking, at a party, silly questions like, Which way is north and Where's the river? — Max is taking another shower and I am sweating in the close room. I listen to the traffic sounds and decide it is morning, early morning, the city coming awake and starting the day. Max comes back wrapped in a towel and fresh for the next round. He puts a large bottle of Glenfiddich on the side table and pours himself a glass. I can smell the whisky. I salivate. He takes a long pull on the liquid and breaks out in a sweat. We are equal for a moment. He gets up and opens the window. The traffic sounds flow in with the cool air. He closes the window, settles himself into the chair next to the whisky. I try to go off into sleep again. He talks. I cannot block the sound. I listen.

'Now Robert's scaling down, getting old, wanting to retire, play it safe in his old age. He really copped the heat in the last ten years — on everyone's lips. Every time there was a slow news week they'd drag out the old photo spread and a bit of the latest gossip for the Sundays. I did a few years inside for that. On his behalf. Well paid. And there's always work to be done in the gaols, running the rackets, keeping the flow of booze and dames and favours going smooth. Lots of junkies inside these days with friends on the outside, what you'd call a captive market eh?' He laughs at his well-worn joke.

When he finally talks about himself it's the dedicated hardworking life, carving a career out of the need for his particular brand of subtle brutality, his perfect obedience to the task. I am deeply impressed by this. I do not doubt his efficiency. Hysteria threatens again. I breathe and breathe. He talks about the breakdown of the old order. 'It's hard to take,' he says, 'after a life of power. Now I'm always looking over my shoulder, having to beat the law, the shifting protections of politicians and cops. And the bloody crims in gaol these days, Jesus, they're talking.'

I think, the backlog of crimes and scandals breaking like old dams behind crumbling concrete walls. If I could speak I would tell him that he suffers from a failure of imagination. Or too much imagination. 'Look at it from another perspective, mate,' I'd say. 'You're bloody lucky, still alive and in one piece. Bet you've got a million or so salted away, tax-free. Why don't you just skip the country?' There must be something ego-tight in there, delusions fixed like tattoos, wanting things to be the same, to be part of it, in the game, still on the make, even when the game's been taken over by the mad and bad of another generation.

He's been talking for hours, and now he's drinking whisky like water, I can hear the slur in his voice and look forward to silence, snoring. But first it'll get maudlin. These guys are so predictable. They watch too much late-night television. They think there's nothing sweeter than an ageing thug with a parodising heart of gold. I resist his bathos, take pleasure in his sudden drunken state and will myself into sleep or trance or unconsciousness. His voice sinks low and he is talking only for himself. I push my anger down into my ankles, making the blood circulate. I am bored and angry and certain that his lowering voice will eventually cease. I study the room inch by inch and then go over it again. I wait my chance.

23. Frances and Solange

On Tuesday evening I drive back to town in the gathering dusk, heading for a dinner date one day late.

Solange. She would remain a name to be passed across my lips like a promise unless I took a few risks.

'Tell me the story of your life,' I said, comfortable as listener.

In the basement of her waterfront home there are three offices and a storeroom full of filing cabinets and storage trunks. A business card captioned 'consultant' can cover a multitude of mysterious doings. Lunch at the Machiavelli on Mondays.

'If I told you where I come from, Wagga Wagga for example, it wouldn't make anything clearer. You want to exhibit photographs, I can fix it. You want to get into the Biennale, I'm your ticket.'

'I don't need any help.'

'You remind me of Ethel Merman singing "Oh you can't shoot a man with a gun".'

'But you can shoot a man with a camera, and you don't need a licence.'

Relax. Pour the wine. Sink back into the chair. Think. This woman likes me. I like her. These differences, this difference.

'I think you are very lovely and I would like to make love with you. There. That wasn't so dreadful.'

I get up from the chair and walk towards her, brush her hair with my hand settling on her shoulder. She's not so relaxed. We kiss.

Later, when Anthony drops around for a brandy, I am waiting for the kettle to boil, the lights are low, I am wearing someone's deep red towelling robe. Anthony calls hello to Solange and takes the brandy bottle into the bedroom. I hear his deliciously thrilled voice. 'It's about time,' he says, never lost for words or enthusiasm.

24. ESCAPE

I wake up. It's quite dark and I hear snoring from across the room. I lean sideways and topple the chair gently to the floor, crawl and push as quietly as I can, slowly, slowly, feeling furniture and surfaces with my face, my forehead, grimacing and straining to free the gag. I hook the sticking plaster on a corner of a table and free my teeth to gnaw. This is not a pretty part of the story. I chew and tear the rope around my shoulders and it loosens across my back, around my arms and I feel my wrists ache with relief. I take precious minutes to free my hands, carefully, silently inching the ropes looser, letting my hands begin to work again. I free my feet and rub them hard. The pain is intense and I am sweating again with the effort to remain very quiet. I crawl away from the snoring, slowly, silently. I pull myself upright against a doorway. I look back at Max, sprawled in the chair, shoes off, legs at full stretch, hands loosely together in his lap. I resist a hard kick to his balls and slip around the doorway and bump into a pot plant. It sways and I catch it, put it gently down and step carefully around it. I am in a hallway with three doors off it — bathroom, kitchen, escape. I open the front door and look out — bright light from the hallway, wide stairway going down, an old block, worn carpet, security front door, leadlight windows, sounds of sleeping and early risers, a toilet flushing, I walk carefully down the stairs, one flight, out the front door, a short pathway, onto the street, no-one around, I smell the air, wait for a sense of direction, something familiar, an instinct, which way to go? Shops on a corner, a road downhill towards the noise of traffic. A taxi passes, I hail it, check my pockets, no money, say, 'Where am I?' The taxi driver looks at me, crumpled, hunched over, clenched tight with shock and shaking like a leaf. He says, 'This is Elizabeth Bay Road and I'm on my way home.' He drives off. I walk back past the block of flats as fast as I can, heading for Solange's place, two blocks away.

25. NOTHING TO SAY

Love affairs are like leaving the country — the take-off is tense but once you're up and flying, it's heady. Time distorts. Senses sharpen and soften, resolve into places and shapes. Feelings and ideas require another language, another culture of pleasure and tension.

When Anne Stevens rings Solange's doorbell at eight o'clock on Wednesday morning we pretend no-one is home. Anthony had been enough of the world last night. After two brandies politely offered and gleefully sipped, he was defeated by our tiny conversation and went off into the night, sated with fresh gossip and his own approval. Anne Stevens would keep.

26. YOU CAN SAY YES AND NO

Deidre has organised a meeting with Louise Andrews. I go into the meeting well-prepared after nights studying company law and financial statements. I insist on an assistant, a financial whiz. He works twice as hard as I do. We begin to make a team.

When Max Cavanagh calls the office I am pleasantly in. He sounds rattled and I send him off to see another solicitor, saying, 'I won't be available Max, no matter what the date.'

PART THREE

Simple present tense

CHAPTER 7

1. FIVE MEN ON TV

The hysteria of summer is over but the weather remains warm, soupy. Winter is postponed and then arrives windy and rough. The air is turbulent. People lean into the wind in the city, clutching umbrellas and hats. Perhaps that's why it took me so long to work things out. That weird weekend. I don't remember whether I was actually kidnapped by Max or just went to sleep and, as they say on the master soaps, it was all a dream. When I woke up I was clear of it all. Very clear. I took a few days off and then went back to the office and put my head down. In the evenings I watched TV, read books, wrote letters, did my tax and cleaned out the cupboards. I was planning on an early spring.

When everything was spotless and ordered I took to staying late at the office. Good work will be rewarded, I told myself. Look after yourself. I tried Frances Smith's number every now and then but she was always out. Then one Friday, she was in and invited me over for dinner. When I arrived she was in a flurry in the kitchen and I drifted towards the living room. There were five men in a row talking on TV. They were lawyers, Royal Commissioners, journalists and campaigners. Between us — she, me, Solange, Harry — we knew all of them. It was great television and it made us feel safe. Our interests were being represented. We could relax now and get on with things — daily life, careers, love affairs.

Frances told me about Solange and I was noncommittal. It's always awkward when your friends fall in love with each other. You know immediately that there will come a day when you cannot speak of the other, and you'll feel irritated and angry that your life is so constrained by the way other people behave. So predictable. She was still in the second, stronger flush of love and did not register my disinterest, my irritation. I told her that Harry was vaguely somewhere but we didn't seem to be seeing much of each other. This was not interesting to her, this old relationship; she made no comment. So I did not tell her that I had closed my life down, that the phone was off the hook and that I was deep in solitude, safety and work. I left early and rushed home, closing the door against the wind. I turned on the television and studied the late news. The five men were on television again. They were talking about corruption, exposure, investigations, structures, commissions, inquiries, reports. They were fluent and enjoying themselves. They had had a number of victories over the years. Their writings were prodigious. Their words were fluid and dreamy, harmonious. They talked to each other; they were confident, excited; they had touched, for brief moments, power, and smelt its heady perfume of fear and attention. They wore very good suits. Some even have wardrobe advisers. One of them had a new pair of glasses. We were asked, with every rational intonation and every ring of moral rectitude, to take their word for it. I watched them with detached fascination. I wanted to believe them and knew in my gut that I didn't.

When winter really arrives the city is at its best. People are swept along by the night, think they are in London or New York, wear hats, stride along wet pavements in stylish boots and great coats, are warm as toast. The nightclubs have gone. Fire regulations ignored for years are suddenly invoked. The doorways are boarded up and gather street litter, homeless people, advertising leaflets. Cafes and dance clubs spring up all over the place; mood music and dancing close come back into fashion. Pop culture predicts the bigger shifts. The bankruptcies start quietly, in ones and twos, and grow. The stock market makes its mark on history but it's not until the property market peaks and falls over that the newspaper columnists will admit some things have gone wrong.

2. Harry

This winter Harry Bean is confident. He moves through the world at an even pace. Smooth, no rush, no panic. He is of medium height, has a medium build and medium routines for keeping fit. He swims, he jogs, he moves around, does a circuit, keeps appointments at a downstairs gymnasium, holds meetings in local parks. Harry Bean feeds the dogs at Lily's place and collects the mail. He jogs back across Dover Heights and down to the harbourside at Vaucluse, checks Max's place in Wolaroi Crescent, passes Robert's place in Vaucluse Road and picks up his car at Nielsen Park. He drives down Fitzwilliam Road — the mansion at number three has recently changed hands and Robert wanted to know the details.

According to the real estate agent Harry met in a pub at Double Bay the new occupants had first sent a woman along to check the place. 'Looked at three on the first day,' the agent revealed after his third Bacardi and Coke, 'bought the third one pre-auction and arranged a super-fast settlement.' They switch to beer. 'Can't tell you how much she paid, mate, the boss is keeping that right under wraps. But I can tell you she moved in last week, supervising the cleaning and decorating.' It was enough to interest Harry Bean. The habits of the rich often threw him a few choice chores, security at parties, driving to Noosa, but Robert would want to know more so Harry scouted his contacts and talked Alex into starting a retaining wall planned for September a few weeks early. Alex landscapes gardens and does a bit of structural work, with and without council permission. Maintenance, cellars, safes, third garages and sandstone retaining walls are his specialties. Encroaching gardens to the foreshore.

Alex puts Harry on the waterfront crew where he lugs loads of sand for the mortar. As he shovels sand into the barrow and wheels it down the ramp and along the two-foot-wide beach to the wall-building thirty metres along, he keeps an eye on the woman and the mansion at number three and ranges his mind across the map of his personal paralegal geography.

'The way I see it,' he might say to himself, 'I am spending time, investing it in small and occasional jobs, hanging out listening and talking, being around, in company, en route, getting out of town, flying interstate, pacing myself.

'It's a bloody full-time job. Doing the rounds, checking the real estate, keeping an eye on too many people and not knowing how any of them will move. And I haven't seen Anne Stevens for months.'

Harry had missed the kidnap scene completely. He'd gone to Melbourne to check out a problem with the nightclubs there, for a friend. The bouncers were getting a rough reputation.

And knowing about Joe Simms didn't help him sleep at night. But telling Frances Smith about it had produced the right outcome. She might not have been shocked but she kept her distance. Harry had felt good about that. He liked to think he was a perceptive social commentator, knowing the story, like the men on TV. 'These days, they say,' he says to the blokes on the site at morning tea time, 'that peak hour at the brothels is before breakfast. These days,' he continues, pausing to accept their attention, 'blokes get up and go out jogging, come back all sweaty, go straight to the bathroom, fill it with steam, grab a quick orange juice and wave to the wife and kids, grab a black coffee standing up at the counter in the Martin Place railway arcade, and on to the office clean as a whistle before the secretaries get in.'

'Yeah Harry, you'd know I reckon.' The brickie is not impressed.

'Don't you jog every morning mate?' Alex asks Harry and the smoko breaks up and the men get back to work hearty with innuendo.

3. FRIENDLY WORDS

Anne Stevens has always assumed her mind liberal and her temperament generous. These things are a matter of pride, and relied upon. At a gracious dinner she has organised for Frances, Solange and Anthony she is struggling to accept the changing status of friendship. Solange is no help. 'We went to this great new venue on the other side of the city last night,' she says. 'People got up and read, listened to other people, actors, reading out, film scripts. It was a very interesting night . . .'

Anne Stevens is amazed, 'You mean to tell me you went along to hear someone read out their film script?'

'No. Actors read it out. Helen Henty's was good. They read the scene notes and shots and stuff. The first half was good. But Bob Richards — Jesus.'

'Why do they do it?' Stevens is struggling to appreciate the joy of this event. 'I mean, do the actors get paid for this?'

Solange is patient, 'So that they can discuss the scripts and work out what's wrong with them.'

Stevens thinks she has gone soft in the head. 'You mean they are reading them out because they're bad scripts, because the films won't get made?

'Well I suppose so,' Solange gives up, 'but that's not the point.'

What had happened to their easy talk? Stevens stops herself from jealousy and pours wine into everyone's glasses. She straightens her shoulders and smiles across the table at Frances and says, 'You know I think there are going to be really big changes in the next few years. They say, you know, lawyers' talk, that these days businessmen have given up visiting the brothels during their early morning jog. Instead, you see these people, up early, out jogging before breakfast, they are meeting their advisers, their lawyers, their accountants, even their bankers. In parks, on street corners. "We could set up an appointment," they say as they glide past. What do you think of that?'

In the appalled silence she realises it is she who is wrong these days. Her silence about Max has made her speech uncertain. It is as if she is swallowing the words back from utterance. Her work on Louise Andrews' case is hard and intense and her professional discussions of it are clipped and emotionless. She has not been out to the gaol for weeks. She has not seen Harry Bean for more weeks. She misses him suddenly. The ache is almost a pain in her groin. She swallows a fish bone and coughs and splutters at the table and has to dash to the kitchen to heave the air into her lungs. Soft white bread. Her chest rises and falls in pain. She drinks water from the tap, glass after glass, as if to ease her throat and let the words come out. She serves strawberries and cream, puts the water on to boil for the coffee.

4. THEY SAY THESE DAYS

There is a beach jogger who does sit-ups at the end of his run with his legs hooked under the chrome hand-rail. By doing his sit-ups like this he manages to look like a big worm. He erects himself in space and sways. Harry is really pissed off with this guy. He is so gauche. No amount of exercise will change his essential pear shape, thin sloping shoulders, thin ankles. He chats up the woman in the latest grey tracksuit. The sunset is Renaissance-painting style with angels on sunbeams, the mist coming down and the spray coming in over the suburbs.

As he runs the length of the beach Harry can feel the promise of spring, can almost smell it coming in off the ocean, as if out there, over the horizon, is a land of certainty, clarity. Soon, the summer, long days, stretched time, calmness, will come. He thinks: things have to get better. He turns to come back up the beach, out there it's only New Zealand.

Harry plunges into the surf at the end of his run. The water is cold and his skin tingles all over. Up on the promenade the worm character showers in the open air, giving himself a brisk towelling. 'I've got a wife and kids and a mortgage,' he is saying to the single woman in the grey tracksuit, who is back again after two lengths of the beach. He and Harry watch the young banker and the young lawyer jog pass talking between puffing. 'We could set up an appointment,' the lawyer is saying.

5. SOLANGE SAID

Solange said, 'The last people who lived in the flat I'm in now told me they were robbed one night. That they woke up one morning to find all the furniture shifted around, that the TV and video were gone, that someone had been playing Trivial Pursuit in the lounge room and that there were puncture marks in their arms. They said they'd been drugged and robbed.'

'Wow.'

'And that they didn't remember a thing about it.'

'They would have felt the needles going in.'

'One of them said it could have been chloroform!'

The evening grinds on.

6. VISITING

I visit Louise Andrews in Mulawa. She has engaged a QC and I take notes, do research. I tell her about my work on her defence in ordinary language. I do not feel immense responsibility.

I ring Harry Bean's mother. She is near eighty and smokes like a chimney. She says she'll get him to ring me next time he checks in, that he calls every day, nearly. I say I can't wait in and could she tell him from me that 'Confusion reigns and danger was visited and returned from, no thanks to him.' She says I am a dear strange girl and seem to suffer from being over-educated, 'But the boy is fond of you, I can tell.'

'Thanks Mrs Bean,' I say, 'that makes me feel really

good.' And I mean it, in my own way, tone of voice as dry as a gangster's eye and half as kind.

7. TAKING TIME

The furniture van that arrives at number three has Victorian number plates. The removalists unload the usual stuff, televisions, leather lounges, crates of linen and crockery, some elaborate sideboards, an immense dining table and many chairs. The beds are ordered new and arrive the next day in a second van from a department store. Harry has nodded and smiled a few times at the woman who appears to be in residence but she never acknowledges his politeness.

The wall job comes to an end. He has discovered nothing much and moves on, picks up a quick week's work placing a few strategic bets and then signs on at Darling Harbour, joining the great workforce assembled to panic-finish the urban park for the following year of celebration. It is good work. Hundreds of carpenters, engineers, plumbers and finishers, fitters and labourers have demolished the vast swampland and industrial docklands bordered by great warehouses from the wool boom. They make a plain beneath the freeways, a plaza where the edge of the city streets run down. They put up new buildings and refit old ones, and there in the middle of the city is a place of curious quiet; beneath the freeways the roar of the traffic is muted. Harry Bean works on the rubbish removal team and graduates to the landscaping, the final touches. But even he is impressed. The landscaping here is something else. Very large-scale. He gets into it, fascinated by the precision of it all. It is like a formal garden and like a vast building without a roof. Articulated vehicles come in relays, each with a full-grown palm tree. Their arrival is perfectly timed, cranes lift, lower, lines are drawn, a row of palm trees takes the eye.

The workers are on short contracts, emergency labour on a job that has already overrun the budget and blown out the debt. There is nothing for it but to keep going — you can't leave a hole in the ground as a symbol of a country's two-hundred-year achievement.

8. Touching wood

I settle to the letter to my father. It is always hard.

> Dear Dad,
> In case anything happens to me . . .

I stop for a long time, reach for a clean sheet of paper but go on.

> I want to tell you a few things. I've been working very hard lately and become all tied up in something I am not entirely sure about. You know me, I always think I know exactly what is what and then it starts to come apart at the seams. Some of it you already know — that big fraud case a month back. And before that I did some work for a chap called Max Cavanagh. He's got quite a reputation, you'll have heard of him. Well, now, this is really hard to say, straight out, I mean it sounds so stupid, but he kidnapped me. I escaped. I'm all right. He didn't do anything to me, but I can tell you, it really scared me.
>
> I can hear what you're going to say. I should have gone to the police. I know, and you know, I couldn't. Not in my position, I couldn't afford the

publicity. And there's the rest. He's a mate of the cops. You know what it's like up here.

There's more. An old client of mine from Melbourne days, Lily Simms (she's related by marriage to that Robert Simms who's been around for decades), she seems to be back in my life, I'm not sure how.

I'm hearing voices again. I haven't told you much about Harry Bean but I will one day. It's an 'approaching-middle-aged-daughter-finds-true-love story', the sort you've been waiting to hear for years. You'll like him, I promise, but the thing is he's tied up in all this and he's gone bush, looking out for himself I suppose, I can't blame him. That's why I'm writing to you, in case anything happens to me, you'll know who to contact and tell this to.

Sorry, Dad. You always did accuse me of melodrama and now I agree with you. But what can a woman do? I'd rather you laugh at me than end up weeping over some bush grave.

Love Anne

9. Right at this moment Harry Bean is

Right at this moment Harry Bean is a bit of a ghost at Randwick Racecourse. He can go to the meetings but no-one speaks to him. He skulks in the half-price enclosure and bets at the TAB. He hasn't been as careful as he should. He'd organised a few mates to lay the fifteen-to-one in the second at Rosehill last week in to five-to-two and watched the favourite go right out to fives and come right in at the post. The last-minute plunge on the favourite in Melbourne, Brisbane and the SP minutes before the race completed the oldest sting in the world and temporarily turned Harry Bean into a ghost. He'd scooped $10,000 from the bank and got to spend a few days at home watching television with the phones turned off and all the blinds down.

He went up to Palm Beach for a week of house-sitting for a friend of a friend and bought his mother a second television set for her bedroom. She would have preferred a dishwasher, she said. He cleared out the David Jones' toy department for the kids he rarely visited and saw the patent anger in ex-wife Sandra's eye and knew he was a bastard and a cheap bastard at that. He took her car off and fitted it out with a set of steel radials, which was something as well as guilt. He'd give her the lot but he knew she would take it. Three kids ate the cash and used the small change for sandcastles. He romped with them in the park for an hour or two, touch football and foot races. He regretted his failure as a father and dropped them back to their mother.

And when he could Harry went back to number three Fitzwilliam Road. On an early morning jog he saw a fit but elderly man come out the front door to collect the paper. The next day he saw the woman who had set the house up drive a car out of a garage. After a week he knew the house was already up and busy at seven in the morning and he saw, switching to a late evening run, that the household went to bed at all hours. There were at least three men; there might have been as many women. The residents came and went, ate an evening meal together, had a servant, a house-keeper at least, and a handy man or odd jobs bloke. The lawns were watered and mowed. There were separate rooms at the back of the house for the help. The woman who had inspected the house came and went — it was hard to tell where she spent her nights.

Harry Bean was not capable of twenty-four-hour surveillance single-handed and he needed money to organise a team. Robert had given no instructions. He didn't follow her. Sometimes she drove the old man when he went out, which was rarely and mostly on race days. The younger men came and went, spending the night at the house or away for days at a time. Harry recognised the pattern, it was so like his own.

Research is what Harry Bean called this casual surveillance. Ten thousand dollars wasn't going to last him beyond a couple of months. Darling Harbour would be finished by the end of the year. The winter was brightening, the days getting longer. An early spring was possible. There was wattle out on the headlands. He liked the set-up at number three. It promised his sort of work. He was ready. Soon, next week, or the week after, he'd phone a mate at Telecom, get the name and number, there was plenty of time. He dropped into his mother's place for dinner and collected his phone messages. None from Robert. One from Anne Stevens. It was about time.

CHAPTER 8

Harry arrives late at night

I lived with a bloke who was a writer once, for a week. That was the first time I learnt the rule, don't read other people's diaries, you will always find out what you don't want to know. I read this bloke's diary and found out: one, that I didn't rate a name, just an initial 'A' or a generalised 'she'; and two, he'd been reading my casenotes: 'She's a terrible writer . . .' — critical glee. There was worse: 'She crowds my space. She sits in the dining room working on her casenotes, writing (my god), pretending to write, humming and speed-reading, the pages flying and I sit in my study, blocked, furious, irritated by her competence, her facility, unable to commit a word.'

That was Alan Jones, suffering for his art and many years ago. Now Harry is passed out on the couch with his paraphernalia spread all over my lounge room and I decide I could do with a refresher course in truth and life's little humiliations. I read his diary. It's not really a diary, not in the lengthy prose sense of Alan Jones' earnest recording of every precious thought and many worthless and contrived ones. But I learned much the same things. One, I didn't even rate an initial or a gen-eralised 'she'. Two, next to my work phone number: 'tame law'. Three, next to my home phone number: 'answer phone'. There weren't many ordinary entries: his mother's phone number and address, various harm-less bureaucracies like the State Library, Computer Services, the Tax Department, Telecom, the Land Register and Long Bay Gaol.

There was a page at the back with his tax file

number, Medicare number and credit union account all neatly recorded. Mr Straight and Narrow, it would seem. There was a dental appointment for August 6 and pencilled dates for car registration and driver's licence renewals. There was a page of telephone numbers, probably crudely coded, or not — how would you know unless you rang them, and then how? I assumed he had the habits of deception. There were other numbers and letters, a more esoteric coding that could have been harmless shorthand for daily doubles or football pools. And there was part of an address, an enticing one, '16 Wallis', not street, ave or lane, no suburb. It was the only address in the book, apart from his mother's, and that made it important. I didn't need to write it down.

There were nine Wallises in the street directory and I spent a day every weekend practising the art of watching and wondering, cruising suburbs I didn't know existed, banking on elimination, guesswork and a sixth sense, an accident, being in the right place at the right time if you like to denigrate such stolid enterprise on my part. Number sixteen Wallis Avenue/Lane/Place/Road/Street. A jealous woman, curious beyond reason, mad in pursuit of nothing. I drove around.

In Strathfield number sixteen was a small park. Out at Mount Pleasant there was no number sixteen. Wallis Glen was a cul de sac on the edge of one of those far out land developments, a few houses built along smooth concrete roads and going off into bush, a likely place for a body, but no number sixteen. In Woollahra, Wallis Lane had ceased to exist and sixteen Wallis Street had been swallowed by the Junction overpass.

Wallis Parade, North Bondi, was a straight road of houses running into the golf course and thence the ocean. Quite splendid. Number sixteen was three from a corner, a free-standing Californian bungalow behind a high fence, padlocks, chains, cyclone wire, concrete, dogs barking. It looked deserted and like its neighbours, curtains drawn. I liked Wallis Place, St Ives. Again a cul de sac, but this time a place of large gardens, tall trees, acres of forest and bushland down to the gully behind. But no number sixteen. I went for a walk in the reserve and listened to all the birds.

Wallis Place, Willmot. The end of the earth is a triangular-shaped suburb out past Blacktown beneath a great freeway, a transmitter station, close to a waste disposal and recycling centre. Number sixteen was a look-alike house on a bare block, washing on the line and a woman, carless, jobless, a single mum with three under six and glad of a chat. Wished I'd had a visit from your Harry or anyone. I love the kids and I'm glad of the house but it gets lonely out here at night with the wind tearing across the plains.

Wallis Street, Leumeah, is another address on the edge. I was beginning to wonder about who this Wallis was — Wallis Simpson perhaps, the ousted, the outsider. Number sixteen was a fibro original from when the suburb had been a rural straggling settlement along the creek and off the main track between Sydney and Camden. The front yard was a clutter of rusted car parts and kids' toys, useful-one-day sets of wheel rims, a rusted swing, sagging cartons of beer bottles. I told Mrs Ristrom about the recycling place across the plains at Willmot and she offered me a cup of tea and called to Ross pottering in the backyard that was a study in contrast: careful vegetables in rows, real tomatoes ripening on the plant and cascades of passionfruit. The front yard debris, it turned out, was a legacy from previous tenants. 'We're gonna leave it like that, it's a sort of museum,' Mrs Ristrom said, happy at last in a house of her own that the young pensioner couple and their two children could afford. 'We're trying to get off the Methadone,' she told me, and I could see the obsessions, the years of addiction, transferred onto the garden. They pressed a basket of produce on me as I left and I took it with real gratitude and real promises to return for a visit soon. I wish I were that sort of person.

I knew I'd found *the* number sixteen when I drove through the National Park to Bundeena and walked along the track to Maianbar. No cars here. A perfect Harry Bean hideaway. I was sure there'd be a number sixteen and there was . . . *and* there was an old man writing his memoirs in retirement and an old woman tending to his every whim and I went away dispirited by her continued homage to his life's work.

These trips and forays passed a month of Sundays. Irrational make-work, the stuff of neurosis-takeover or exhaustion or determination. It is now late winter. The spring winds have come early. The weather is freezing, deceptive blue sky and sunshine and the wind reaching through to the skin. I had planned to walk along the cliff top from Watsons Bay to Bondi, check out the Wallis Parade house again, as a sort of punchline to this longwinded joke of my curiosity. The jealousy has gone with the miles. It is not a sustained character flaw. I think of it more as a sign of normality. Despite the free love of the sixties and the non-monogamy of the seventies, jealousy reminds me that I value others, lovers, and myself. That meaning still exists beyond the moment or pleasure or whim. I like Harry Bean. I like his body and his cracked face and his no-bullshit bravado. I don't like his absence.

I park the car on the corner of Wallis, Wairoa and Blair. There's a big sea crashing on the rocks at North Bondi and no surfers, a few intrepid walkers bundled up in coats and scarves determined, like me, keeping their rituals going. I have a good view up the street to the golf course. I can see the flame of the sewerage works across the roof tops. The street is quiet, Sunday afternoon. I wait.

Numbers sixteen, eighteen and twenty stand behind their high walls, blinds drawn, an acre of concrete and yards of cyclone wire. Identical houses carefully anonymous. Dogs barking at kids on bicycles pushing uphill with a head wind, cruising back down. The sounds of orchestral music come with the bluster of the wind. A car pulls up to number eighteen and the gates open to a remote control, the car disappears into a garage. I stand across the street. I stand at the gate of number sixteen. I press the buzzer. The airwaves open with a crackle but no-one speaks. I say, 'I'm a friend of Harry's.'

I watch the house. The silent blinds, the unmoving concrete, the prowl of the dog back and forth behind cyclone wire. Lily Simms opens the door. I follow her along a concreted passageway and into a surprising expanse of lawn, a well-established bush garden fragrant with wattle, boronia and early jasmine, an expanse of paving, a pool, a terrace with glass doors from three houses, the sound of orchestral music, the distant barking of a dog.

CHAPTER 9

There are times in your life

There are times in your life when you stop worrying. I walked into Lily Simms' backyard on that blustery Sunday afternoon in late autumn 1990 and I stopped trying to figure out the world. I didn't make mental notes. I didn't watch what I said. I didn't set up each sentence as if it were a time bomb. Something had happened. I'd gone, on my nine visits to nine streets called Wallis, past some point of rational behaviour and it had paid off. It had given me the goal I did not know I had been seeking. I had been wanting to talk to her again. The perfectly balanced equation.

I remember thinking, 'Right,' and 'I get it' and grinning and Lily Simms looking back at me, her smile broadening. 'A friend of Harry's,' she said, 'I'm not sure who that's a compliment to or who it's a reference for. Anne Stevens, a little ghost from my past. Everything pays out its capital, every debt is finally called in, wouldn't you say?'

I said nothing. The garden was protected from the south wind and the sun shone like spring. A small fortress in suburbia. The backs of the houses on the street behind, boarded up, eyeless. No flats overlooked this patch.

'Harry didn't tell me you were coming.'

'Harry doesn't know. I . . . I've been on a long search for you . . .' I let myself smile at the absurdity of my quest.

We sit in a north-facing room, the warmth of sun through glass. It is a formal sitting room. She offers coffee. I accept. Old times threaten to re-establish patterns. I make a business of finding cigarettes and lighter, look around for an ashtray.

'Do you want me to have a word with Max? He's having a bit of trouble settling on reality these days, I hear. Nothing serious.'

I think about my night of captivity, the absurdity of that. I didn't tell anyone. Not even Harry. But she knows. I find my voice, 'He's having a mid-life crisis. He told me all about it.'

'All about it?'

'As much as he can keep straight in that addled brain of his. Is it booze or is he on something else? Or is that what they call "blood simple"?'

'All of that. It's not an easy life, you know. They work as hard as merchant bankers or stockbrokers or company directors, and for less in the end. No golden handshake, and no corporate lawyers sorting out the details while you "rest up" in Tahiti and wait for the fuss to die down.'

Lily Simms looks long and hard out the window. 'It's not much, is it,' and it's not a question. 'Something, but not much for all I've copped from those bastards over the years.'

A small fortress. A small fortune. No security. A widow with a record. Middle age approaching. If she'd been a random number sixteen Wallis Street out in the western suburbs I would have been sympathetic. Why wasn't I now?

Lily Simms could have marked her life in men or hairstyles, cars she's owned or the legal and illegal addictions she's worked at and thrown. She could have marked her life by the births of children: the first pregnancy breezy; the second casebook morning sickness and some unknown hospital ward in Melbourne she'd left after a day; the third, at home, not by desire, a fast labour and alone in the house, Joey off somewhere and not coming back. She'd crawled to the telephone and got Ruth to call an ambulance and when it came the boy was slimy and warm on her breast, a special child who came in the daylight and insisted, love me enough by yourself, a premonition.

Joey had always been a problem. Lily never let herself think about that. Joey had been there, a fixture, a friend. Two friends in a fix, that's what he called them. 'Fixing to make it out of here one day and into the promised land. Stick with me, kid. We'll see Broadway at dawn.'

Broadway Sydney at dawn was a miserable place and she'd seen it the night Joey's mate had been shot in a lane by a gun-happy cop and she'd seen it coming from the overnight train from Melbourne back after long years of exile with the kids cranky-tired and the sun hot and steamy on their Melbourne winter coats, saturated with the air of people asleep together in an enclosed space, snoring, farting, burping, simply digesting, encrusted, sweating, extruding, giving off the smell of endurance. And she'd seen it from across the street staring up at the newspaper offices when they'd blasted her face all over the front page and she'd been going to go in and say something to the editor about her kids in school and her right to live in peace.

Moments of strength and weakness, of the past, gone. Lily Simms marked her life in real estate. Warehouses. Offices. Clubs. Premises. Houses. The enclave in a street of enclaves.

At our second meeting Lily was bleak in the beachside cafe, spoiling the view with grey and frown. She said I was out of danger. A small player. I got the message, am in her debt. She said she would be going away for a while. 'Good,' I had said, 'you look like you need a holiday.' She had laughed, shook her head. As she went to the counter to pay the bill she said, 'It's a clean slate, OK? No debts.'

The Woollahra police phoned Lily at nine-thirty to say they would be around at midday. They had a series of forged cheques and bank photographs dated and ID'd. She'd been neatly fingered. It was a routine matter. Lily phoned her lawyer. A real lawyer. A bloke who knew the law and the police and the procedures and would play every move correctly. Lily was not looking for trouble, publicity or even an acquittal. She'd cop the play. There was a reason for it. She would find that out later. For now she had to arrange for someone to collect the children from school, to take them to their grandmother's and explain her absence. Harry would feed the dogs without question. Robert would find out from the word around town. If she played it cool and quiet the papers would miss it until she came up for trial and then they'd think she was just the hard-up widow of the recently deceased.

Lily packed a bag she wouldn't need and waited with a hot pot of coffee for the detective sergeant and his offsiders to appear smoothly in her lounge room to escort her to the newly-built police centre where she would suffer two days of sensory deprivation.

It was ten years or more since Lily Simms had been inside but when she arrived at the remand section of the gaol it was as if nothing had changed. Most of the women were in for drug-related offences — possession, using, dealing, the courier trail — or for cheques, like herself, or fraud, credit cards, the ocassional bashing, one or two charges of murder. The food was, if anything, worse, the coffee/tea was the same old ersatz confusion. Lily took up smoking again in a mild sort of way so that she would have something valuable to bargain with.

Louise Andrews had been three months on remand — she was an old hand by now. She had taken all advice on offer, had learned to talk without the upward inflection. In gaol you don't ask questions, you make statements and you make direct eye contact. Every exchange is a test of your belief in yourself. She smoked Lily's brand, offered an afternoon cigarette, made cups of tea. She had developed a nice fantasy to make it all bearable — I didn't really do it, I am innocent and will be released soon. This was tiresome to listen to. Lily switched off and watched her hands. They made small pushing motions, as if she was smoothing a sheet on a bed or swimming an uncertain and ladylike breaststroke. Was she a swimmer caught in a rip? Lily remembered teaching her own children what to do if they got caught in a rip. The advice: swim across the current, don't try to swim against it. Or go with it, out to sea, it will bring you back somewhere else eventually.

CHAPTER 10

Looking for someone

In the last six months I have taken many photographs of views, buildings, faces. I say I am working on a series, sea views of course, photographs of the marvellous old seawater baths that were built along the coast in the Depression and are still functioning. I come near to the end of the series, Maroubra, and discover someone else has done it before me and put out some very stylish, hand-coloured postcards that are selling well in Oxford Street art shops.

I decide that people in Sydney have terrible dogs. Even the purebreds are somehow ugly and wrong-looking and the bitsers are really weird. I start taking surreptitious photographs of these dogs that I come across in the street. They are great. I love them. I laugh a lot at them but when I show them around people look at me and say calendar and chocolate box. The worst response is: 'Why didn't you include the owners? You know, all that stuff about how people start to look like their pets.' People in Sydney are so serious.

Perhaps it is the light. In Victoria, in Melbourne where I come from, being so far south, the light is really different. It is sharper, more white and black. In Sydney the light is yellow, the night is brown, golden-black. This is the subtropics. In the south, in the real crisp cold of the winter and the real blasting heat of the summer, there is a sharp edge to things. Next thing I'll be sitting up with the whisky bottle as company and writing morbid letters to old lovers. Or mushy ones to the new.

I spend the winter in love and in looking for work.

This is my preferred lifestyle. I talk on the phone, I make calls, I leave messages, I drink coffee in fashionable cafes and walk for miles to save on bus fares and keep fit. I cook, I spend mornings at the markets buying everything fresh, I make feasts, I go away for the weekend, I stay on alone for a couple of days, I panic about love and work and run to the train station to return. In the city in a rush the sun is shining and the August breeze is warm. I stride off across the park behind the station and arrive at the house in a sweat. There are a thousand urgent telephone calls for me I am surprised. I ring the numbers in random order. The *Daily Sun*'s Joanne Drape is third on the list. 'You don't know me,' she says, 'but Solange gave me your number.'

'Yes,' I say, 'what can I do for you?'

The job is impermanent, part-time, freelance. In fact it might not be a job at all — taking shots on short notice, waiting for the daily call-out, night and early morning work. 'Are you interested?'

So these days I take photographs for the newspapers, a no-credit deal, selling every pretension to art and seriousness for great action shots — the tennis, the football, the police car crashed into the power pole, the body face down in a pool of blood in some nameless street out west. The pool of blood.

SLIDES:

You find someone and are surprised to discover that you were looking. The first photograph shows me, standing straight-on to the camera, feet a foot or so apart, arms hanging at my sides. It is a deceptively plain stance; it is a stance of readiness.

Here is a photograph Solange took of me. It is first thing in the morning. I am bad-tempered, in a hurry and not one bit impressed. I am grabbing for the camera as she shoots. I look like a frantic fish out of water or someone with a thyroid problem. I am probably both.

Here is a photograph I took of Anthony, Terence and Solange walking arm in arm in arm along George Street. They are in full stride and have a lovely look in their eyes. Each of them smiling, soft, in joy.

I develop these photographs at work where the dark-room is first-class and free. I come home and put the last one in a frame and put it on the mantelpiece in my rented Redfern room. I go through a week's mail and come to a postcard from Anne Stevens. I telephone. She is in. I say, 'You sound like you are a very long way away.' She says, 'Is that better?' I hear her cough, clear her throat, and her voice comes up louder, stronger, 'Can you come for a meal or something?'

I drive out as the sun sets. The days are getting longer — spring will come early this year. It is still cold in the night and misty in the mornings but the edge of winter has gone from the city and I drive out around the harbour bends and curves with my window down and the salt wind on my skin.

There is a lot of talk about friendship and trust and doing things for other people and the upshot of it all is that Stevens wants me to go out to Mulawa to visit Lily Simms for her. Saturday afternoon. 'Send your friend,' she says her friend Louise Andrews had said her friend Lily Simms had said.

Lily Simms had been more specific. 'When you talk

to Stevens,' she had said to her new friend Louise Andrews, tell her I want to see her friend, Frances Smith. The one with the camera and the famous father. I'm going to need something special to deal with this.'

Anne Stevens doesn't know all of this. In any case she is more interested in telling me about Harry Bean's mysterious absences than about Louise Andrews and Lily Simms meeting up in gaol, although later she says, 'The last time I saw her Lily said she was going away. I didn't know she meant gaol. She didn't tell me.'

Then she says, 'I got a call from my father this morning. You know how he hates to use the phone. But I wrote him a letter and he rang me straight away. He's a darling sometimes, but he wasn't being kind or concerned — he said he wanted to tell me something, could I come down? What do I do, Frances? I can't say no. He never asks, and I can't leave right now, everything is too . . . imminent.'

I say I'll make the visit and that she is free to leave town. I go to the gaol to visit someone I have never met but recognise from photographs. We sit across from each other and she says, 'Did you bring any smokes?' and I hand over the carton of Winfield and the warden comes up and says, 'Two packets only.' I pass the two packets over and keep the rest in my lap. We play a game of keeping up the conversation and sleight of hand — she stashes the smokes in her trousers and I pass the rest of the carton over two at a time.

'I'm Lily.'

'I've heard of you. I always thought you were one of Stevens' imaginary clients. Too good to be true.'

'I'm real all right and I want you to get me out of here. Robert Simms, my husband's brother, he's behind this.' She gestures at the prison visiting room.

I say 'Yes?'

'There's money, property. I have a lot of control.'

'Control?' I say. 'You're in here and he's holding all the aces,' I say.

She smiles. 'I'm in here and I've been here before but I've got kids in care in some godforsaken place in the country and I've got a lot of money if only I could get my hands on it.'

'Safe deposit box?'

'Commonwealth. Double Bay. And private security.'

'Keys?'

'Later. Next week. You come and visit me again. But first, find out what Robert's got at the house. There might even be something that could help Louise Andrews. She's a bunny, that one. Seems half happy.' She cuts her diversion short. 'But I know there's evidence that would make your skin crawl. I collected a lot of it. You get in there, look under *L* and *W* and *E*. Landscape gardening. Waste disposal. Efficiency. It's all there.'

'And what do I do with it? Go to the police? That's a bit unlikely don't you think?'

Lily stared at me. 'Get the evidence and come back and tell me all about it. And don't involve Stevens. She's not to be associated.'

Lily Simms spoke low and fast: the plan of the house, the security system, the number of the safe, Robert Simms' Sunday afternoon routine. This was a scene familiar from my childhood — the social day, lunch with selected friends, the regulars, an interstate guest or two, the men retiring to the library for cigars and whisky and talk in the late afternoon. I listened hard and sat on quietly in the emptying room when time was called. Anne Stevens was going to call me when she arrived in Victoria. 'How do you feel about break and enter?' I could ask her, knowing the answer and knowing it is something to be done without discussion.

CHAPTER 11

Frances Smith and Harry Bean
do not tell each other everything

Harry Bean is waiting on the seat at the bus stop on the corner of Pitt Street when I come back from seeing Lily. I might not have noticed him at all except that I had to go up to the laundromat to collect my washing and dry cleaning. Perhaps he was waiting for someone else. Redfern is full of small shops and front rooms turned into curtained clubs. The barber shop over the road is a post-box. I know this because I have seen the Rolls-Royce stopped outside on Monday mornings as I go, just as regularly, to the corner shop for the milk.

Harry Bean and I walk the length of Pitt Street to Prince Alfred Park. We go right by my house without so much as a glance. It is a still mild winter afternoon and we sit in the park looking towards the tennis courts and the railway and the city beyond. We sit there as the chill comes down and the sunset turns the city buildings to liquid gold. We watch the tennis matches go on under lights.

'What I don't understand is not what's going on, but is anything going on? We've all become a bit intense.' I begin to talk in general terms, hoping to catch something to make a key turn in a lock.

'The trouble is you keep expecting it to make sense, like a serial moving tortuously slow through the labyrinth of side plots and byways towards an order, a clarity, a closed book.'

'You mean, there's no honour among thieves?' I play dumber than I am and he isn't stupid. We sit in silence.

He decides something and begins to speak with calm precision.

'They were all together, Robert, Joey, Lily, Max, but remember it wasn't for long, a year, eighteen months at the most, and then Joey had to leave town. He came back maybe two years later, he worked for maybe another eighteen months, then he was gone. The story isn't a story as such, it's a series of gestures, accidents, moves. These guys are businessmen. They make plans. When I came up to Sydney, years ago, before any of this was happening, Robert was a real lair. He ran the clubs real close to the edge. But there were manners, codes, set pieces if you like. The boss sat behind the desk and the front men, or women, took the flak. It was a high old time, I tell you, when the Americans were in town on R and R from Vietnam, when the governments changed and things got rearranged, but definitely arranged.'

I want to interrupt this tired, nostalgic rave. It's an old story, told over and over again, as if the telling can return the order and the pleasure of the past. I sit patient and attentive. Optimistic. I intend to work for Lily Simms. There might be something.

Harry goes on with his tale: 'Then there's some weird shift, like a slow explosion. Robert's out of the clubs, he's working real estate and building sites. Then Joey lobs, the edge comes a bit closer.

'Things change. You don't even know they are changing and then one day you can't remember how it was any other way. Years later, there might be an inquiry, a coroner's report, lawyers with elaborate questions. Robert had a routine. Say the licensing boys would try something on, the lawyers would go into action. Years later, and I mean years, when the reports were published, Robert had got rid of the clubs, inflation took care of the fines. He'd expanded into drugs for a time, did some waste disposal for tidy sums. Good cash flow, low overheads — find a manhole and pour the stuff down.

'You wouldn't believe how that guy can move. I remember this one, but he was always doing it. He had the idea one night when the papers were screaming headlines and dragging out all the old photos. The next day a complete set of plans of the stormwater systems of the city were delivered. He hired trucks. We drove them. He hired a garage, sat in the front office for two months, answered the phones, took the orders, worked out the shifts, the routes, the dumping points.

'We worked mostly at night, used to end up out at the Flemington Markets. You could park the truck and get a shower and a pile of bacon and egg rolls. Robert wanted to branch out into straight vegie delivery but we drew the line at that, it wasn't cool.

'The thing is, the thing I want to tell you is, he set up the system and moved on. You hear things, that he sold the rights to illegally dump industrial waste for half a million dollars. We were off the road the next day and sitting around the Palm Beach place, throwing ideas around. We were still there when Drummer Sinclair sailed into Coffs Harbour and walked down the gangplank into the welcoming arms of the police. They had driven fast without stopping all the way from Sydney to Coffs to make the arrest. It took them five and three-quarter hours.

'Robert attended Drummer's court case. He went every day of the prosecution. He'd sit in the back of the court for a few hours. A presence.

'Then the call came through. The cops were on

the line. They'd picked up the kilograms of heroin Drummer had dropped into the ocean for them. They were looking for distribution. Remember that photograph of Drummer on the front of *The Sun* a few years back? You'd have loved it. The detectives are taking him away from the yacht for questioning and he is laughing with one of them. Perhaps he is telling him about getting rid of Lance Doyle along with the dope, or one of his other specialties. Who knows?'

I try and carry my part of the conversation but I have to fight to be interested. 'So these days, who knows, there's another shift on?'

'The point,' Harry says, 'is that Max and Robert are not about to lose the game. They'll have a plan and we'll all find out what it was in about seven years time. When it's history.'

He has told me nothing and I return the favour. I do not tell Harry Bean about Lily and her plans. But then Harry Bean does not tell me about the new residents in Fitzwilliam Road. Neither of us mention Anne Stevens. 'What exactly do you want?' I ask finally and he says nothing for a long time, deciding not to tell me things. I say, 'I don't really want to go on talking in riddles. It's getting cold. I've got things to do.' He sits with his forearms on his knees. It is a clenched and tense pose. It is the body of a serious man working at silence. He is uncertain.

But I am bored. I say, 'It's attractive, becoming the detective. The whole seduction of the role is a cure for the urban blight of alienation, loneliness and fear.'

'The detective is never alone,' I continue. 'He never has to worry about finding someone to talk to, never has to romance the object of desire. No buying flowers or waiting for the phone to ring. The "other" is always

155

interested. The detective is always ready. The only thing that has to be overcome is the detective's reticence. In this sense it is a classic romance — the detective is coy, the other, the liar, the cheat, the betrayer, is ravenous, strong, desirous.

'The detective is in doubt, questioning the morality and worth and goodness of the other, a puritan prig with a prick in a permanent state of tumescence. He is always a great stud, by implication.'

Harry Bean waits for me to finish. I wait for him to respond. The park is floodlit for another safe night in the city and the air is very cold, crisp and still. We walk back to the house and sit in the kitchen with a bottle of wine breathing. I cook.

Harry Bean says, 'My job is to make sure the parts do not come together. The trick is to make sure all the players keep their distances. There will never be a cosy meeting of Max, Lily and Robert to sort out the details of the business.

'Robert likes to keep Max on the hot spot. Max is an expendable player and he knows it. He knows a lifetime of secrets and enough of the financial side of the business to pose a certain threat, informer perhaps, a place on the witness protection programme. But that is a poor alternative for Max, who does have a wife and kids kept pretty secret and safe up in the Hunter Valley and who has a taste for a leisurely retirement where he can abandon the city altogether and, he imagines, his memories and stories of fearful nights and bloody murder as well as the long slow months and years of gaol done variously and always for a tidy sum paid out at the end. Robert isn't sure. Max seems to be losing his grip on the way things are — Robert the boss, Max the worker, Robert the respectable, Max the one who takes the rap and deals with the dirty work.

'Lily knows that Robert is all-powerful, that Max is a thug who will be beaten one day and that she, Lily, is younger, experienced, hard as nails, sharp as a tack, as solid as a rock and a pillar of strength. Her endurance is universally admired. Her poise in front of the newspaper hacks, the crude television cameras rushing to meet the news deadlines, is legendary. She has become someone, a widow with a past, an ex-husband ex-hit man gone missing. She has a sort of power, the power of simply being there, and the power of blood.

'Robert is careful of her, generous, respectful, controlling. She is another buffer for him against the ravaging hordes of pretenders, fast-livers and bully-boys who come into the business, the life, and want to make their mark. Her enigmatic peripheral existence lends his business a serious edge. She does not go about much but her appearance at a club or a racetrack is enough to signal that Robert is interested, will know.'

I say, 'Robert knows that Lily is in gaol. He put her there. But he does not know about me. He knows about Anne through Max but he does not know about Anne and you. Lily knows all about Robert, a bit about Anne, quite a bit about me, courtesy of yourself. She is in the first position. You, I say, know about all of them, and more, all that you are not telling me, but you don't have any power. You are not the detective because your power is in keeping the pieces separate, discrete, edgy, moving, the machine in its parts, well maintained, oiled, purring, going on.'

Harry Bean says, 'I am not the detective; I am on the way out.'

I say, 'I am not the detective; I am part of the plot.'

157

We drink more wine. 'If Anne Stevens were here,' I say, 'what would she say?'

'Well,' says Harry, thinking carefully, 'she'd say, "I am not the detective . . . I am an advocate".'

'And an adversary,' I interrupt, 'committed entirely to the side that is paying . . .'

I am in turn interrupted. 'She'd say,' said Harry Bean with slow drunken glee, '"I am not the detective, I charge too much".'

He is pleased with himself but I am ready for him to leave. I start doing the dishes and he helps me with the drying up. I wish someone would come home and take him off my hands. I am exhausted by the day and the task at hand. I refuse to make him coffee and ask him to drive me across town. I don't tell him where I am going. The habits of the double life come back to me like mother's milk, like father's hands. He drops me in the Cross and I walk down to consult with Solange.

CHAPTER 12

1. IT IS ALWAYS AN EPIC JOURNEY

It is always an epic journey to visit my father: I take the first plane out of Sydney, a taxi from the airport to the station. I catch the train to Frankston and then the local bus to a block away from where my father lives. I arrive in the late afternoon. He is waiting on the front verandah and comes down to the gate to greet me and carry my suitcase. He is more than pleased to see me and hugs me hard. 'It's good to see you girl.'

We settle to a cup of tea before the usual tour of the garden but this time he is jumpy, waiting for me to drink. When I pour a second cup he becomes exasperated. 'All right, girl, you just sit there and have a look at these.' He goes into the lounge room and comes out with a new manila folder. I begin to look through the press clippings as he speaks. 'I've been up at Russell Street, helping the police. They've got him. They've got him at last. I saw this one in the *Sun*.' He pulls out a two-paragraph filler. 'I thought about it for a day and then I contacted them. They've got him at last.'

I read fast:

THE STAUNTON MUTILATION MURDERS SOLVED

The twenty-year-old murders of Stella Newman and Barry Green at Staunton were solved this week with the arrest and charging of one Arthur Simpson, currently on sentence in Pentridge prison for rape and known as the Eastern Suburbs Rapist. A police spokeswoman said the latest charges had come about through a combination of diligent matching of witness statements and new forensic techniques.

A longer article backgrounds the cases. I read it although I need no reminding of even one detail. But I'm interested to see how it is described:

The brutal murders outside Staunton in January 1965 are amongst the most gruesome and puzzling cases police have had to deal with. Green and Newman were well-known teenagers. The mutilation killings which occurred in bushland 10 km east of Staunton in January 1965 shook the close-knit rural community.

Simpson, a one-time farmer from Staunton East, had apparently moved to Melbourne when his wife, living under an assumed name, left him after years of domestic violence and brutality. The former Mrs Simpson's whereabouts are a closely guarded secret. She does not talk to the press and did not give evidence at the rape trial. It is believed that she will be called as a witness at the murder trial, as she and Simpson were still living together at the time he allegedly committed the murders.

My father says, 'I'm going up again for the trial, in December they think. I want you to come with me. We'll see justice done after all this time.'

I look up at him and he is beaming, not smiling or grinning but sort of glowing, triumphant. His life has been resolved. The mystery is revealed. Some sicko maniac with a lifetime of rapes and murders and wife-beating and child abuse, and his own abused childhood to complete the picture. I look at my father and feel like weeping. All those women, those kids, all those lives messed up and ruined and made untenable — my father's included, although that is of a different order. I want to say this to him but don't. He is purged of something, the years of horror and guilt. He says, 'I knew who it was, you know, but there was nothing I could do.'

I look at him long and hard. He believes himself. That is the difference between us. I believe I can do something.

2. I GO BACK OUT TO THE GAOL

I go back out to the gaol. I need more information, specifics. Lily is very up; she's had her hair cut and she's walking and sitting tall. She looks stately, like one of those successful matrons in a department store who attract the best of service without so much as an eyebrow raised.

She begins in the middle of the conversation: 'Robert's place has an elaborate alarm system. Approach from the sea, cut the power supply, take torches. The safe is in the office on the ground floor. You enter from the library.'

'I know how to pick a lock but I'll need the combination to the safe.'

'At least you won't have to blow it up.'

'What's in it for you?'

'He's a meticulous bastard, reckons some day they'll let him write his memoirs, you know the story, me, Joey. Joey's dead, me here. There might be something. Look around — '

'What am I looking for? It won't have your name on it. Colour coding seems a bit simple. Somehow I don't believe you. Here, have another packet of cigarettes, Silk Cut, more feminine. I guess you cut it just fine in this place, old friends, that sort of thing.' She stares back, shrugging into the smile. I am pissed off — back in the middle of it, a Smith at heart, and she'd picked me a mile off.

3. I STAY WITH MY FATHER

I stay with my father for three nights, five days. I scrub out the kitchen cupboards and we go on a day trip to the Frankston shopping mall and buy up on under-wear, a cardigan, slippers and a couple of good shirts. For him. We buy good baked pasties from the bakery and a bottle of chianti for our last night together. We are very sophisticated and enjoy ourselves and each other. I feel like a parent with a child. He feels like a parent who is allowing his daughter to feel like a parent with a child. We enjoy our separate benefits from this ordinary playing of roles. He allows me to drive. I allow him to open the wine. We both allow each other to talk and laugh and get a little drunk. We are celebrating something after all, even if what we are celebrating — his redemption, his rehabilitation, at the age of seventy, after all this time — is about waste and lost living and terror.

I lose another day travelling back to Sydney and read the newspaper reports of the Arthur Simpson case in a coffee shop where I go by taxi straight from the airport. I do not want to be back in the city just yet.

I leave my suitcase with the cafe owner and catch a bus in Oxford Street out to Bondi Beach. I get off the bus at the south end and walk along the beach through the dark. At the north end I climb up past the Club and turn downhill in sight of the golf course. I press the bell in the fence at Lily's enclave. If I've timed it right . . . Harry answers the door. 'Just feeding the dogs while she's away,' he says, and I follow him inside.

162

I say, 'I'm glad you're here. I wanted to see you but I wasn't sure how to do it. We seem to have missed each other lately.'

He wasn't going to respond. Men like him don't. They have no practice at ordinary conversation — it's all lines and scoring points with them. The stuff that makes them attractive in the first place ends up making them impossible in the end. I couldn't even begin. Was it the absence that threw me or the connections? I felt like I had been used but I didn't know what for. I thought Harry Bean and I had a good casual relationship, you know the sort of thing, nothing spoken but a lot more understood. I'm one of those women, I have no aptitude for ordinary conversation with men — it all sounds like a text book or a bad interior novel if I try it.

What about commitment? the Americans would say. It's all about commitment. His refusal to commit was the problem. I didn't want commitment, I wanted continuity, relaxation, being able to assume, assumptions, the going on. But it's hard to go on having a love affair when you never see the other person.

But I was seeing Harry Bean now and I honestly wasn't sure that I wanted to love him.

Love is not an issue. I leave. I am dismayed by this. There is something unfinished and it's not just a love affair. I leave Harry at Lily's place with an ambiguous 'See you later'. I am not dismayed; I am disarrayed, out of order, untidy. I need to tidy up a few things, make things safe and clear for myself before I can go back with any sort of panache and pleasure with sweet Harry Bean who, interrupted in his house-minding and pet-sitting, remained monosyllabic. 'See you.'

CHAPTER 13

Cordless telephone land

I had been gone only a few days but when I arrived back in Sydney it was as if a definite social change had taken place. Men were standing in the streets talking into portable telephones, pacing a piece of the footpath like it was wall-to-wall Berber. They were sitting in cafes talking loudly in these telephones. Their companions tried not to listen. Privacy had been abolished. Offices were no longer necessary. I had returned to a cartoon city where Nail Art and kerbside deals defined the culture. I started to walk from Bondi to Watsons Bay and gave up half way and hailed a taxi. The house smelled of the past and I opened all the windows and lay down on the floor and tried to relax. It wasn't going to let up. Harry cold. My father telling himself stories. Lily and Louise still in gaol. Frances Smith was out and I couldn't bring myself to phone around.

I arrived at Solange's place and she welcomed me effusively. 'I need someone to talk to,' I said but she gushed on regardless. I'd never seen her anything but cool and calm. She ran on, 'What is the point of all the laws and commissions and inquiries that go on endlessly rising and declining?' This is my territory, I might have something to say, but I am not given a chance.

'They are like great waves on the ocean that come so far they fade out miles from shore and make a gentle swish on the sand when they land.' She comes to rest as if surprised by her images, takes a breath, sets her brow in furrows, ploughs on, 'The waves of corruption fade out as they approach the business of charges and incarceration.'

164

'Anthony made a fortune out of the Black Deaths in Custody Royal Commission,' I say quickly. 'That is the way things go.'

She rushes on, 'Don't be glib and easily cynical. That is exactly my point. Don't you see all this retrospective documentation and superficial and stern reports aren't a deal or a game, they are a system of protection that is perpetrated by the very system that affects to document, disclose. Those five men were on TV again last night, reassuring.'

She might have a point or two but I am in a state and not up to the academic argument. 'It will all come out in the end,' I say with facility. 'There'll be a new round of inquiries and commissions "in place".' I am alarmed by this frenetic Solange babbling at me near hysteria.

I say, 'On my way from the airport to Bondi I saw five separate men standing on the street making telephone calls from mobile phones. They could be anywhere.'

'They have to be within a certain distance,' Solange responds, back on her efficient track for a moment. Then, 'In five years time,' she says, 'those five men, the ones on TV not the ones on the street, will be gone, onto other things, premature retirement, private enterprise, investment, the Bar. One might even be pointing at maps while the war winds up. "Good one, Sir."'

'And,' I say, always entertained by a paranoid fantasy, 'the five men on the cordless telephones will be bankrupt.'

'Owing money in all directions and swimming across the rip.' Solange was back in the water, relieved I had taken up her refrain. We subsided and we sat in a sort of blustery silence, sipping wine and reaching for cigarettes. Frances Smith sped into this quiet anxiety and we breathed out again. She did a double take when she saw me but it did not take the triumph from her entrance or the heat from her explosive presence.

'Anyway . . .' Solange made as if to continue. Frances Smith stared at her for a while with fascination. 'Anyway,' Solange began again, but this time with a broad smile on her face and a deep breath of relief, 'you're back safe and sound. I have prevented Anne Stevens from discovering our little plot.' She turned to me, 'You might have felt moved to phone the police or summon your mate Harry to the rescue.'

I lean back into the sofa and refrain from drumming my fingers on the side table. They call each other darling and string out the enigmatic scene for a few minutes. I wait for a break in the duet. 'OK Frances Smith, you've got a story to tell. This better be good.'

'Beyond even your wildest imaginings, my friend.' She is enjoying herself. 'For you I will start at the beginning.

'Getting the aerial shots of Robert Simms' house wasn't hard. The real estate market has been climbing hysterically. There've been amazing scenes — agents tripping over each other to urge more and more buyers to ask for higher and higher prices. The deals are spectacular. The agents are becoming the new rich, they're on the A List, the glossies have been writing in-depth feature articles on them. It's a great time for photographing houses.

'That casual, on-call freelance photography job I have turned into a full-time eat-your-life-up, do-anything-go-anywhere-for-not-much-money sort of thing with the promise of a staff position next time there was a vacancy. The real estate airlift is a regular

Thursday event — at the helipad at six a.m. please, though we spend the first hour of the day wolfing down bacon and egg sandwiches and thick milky coffee and yarning about the millions behind today's jobs. Our pilot doubles as a traffic commentator on the early radio shift and likes to be finished by ten, whence he retires to an early opener for another breakfast and stumbles home to sleep before the afternoon peak-hour. He has a routine and none of us like to suggest he change it so we swoop out over the bridge and follow Military Road out to Mosman for the four bedroom three baths with water views, then west to Parramatta and follow the Parramatta Road back in at seven-forty-five exactly, shooting sidelines, bird's eye views of concertina accidents and bottlenecks on the freeway entrances. We go south at the city and start the home run at Malabar, swooping over Bondi Beach for a bit of fake shark spotting, dipping down over Dover Heights where new mansions are built over the top of ordinary bungalows. They look like postmodern pop-up books. Down round the harbour's east side snapping the great mansions of the rich that are changing hands and acquiring noughts at the rate of knots.

'Last Thursday we hovered above the exclusive peninsulas, fingers into the harbour. Treed and gardened, terraced and piered, water frontages, sweeping lawns, a jetty leaning on three piers — there, that one, Robert Simms' place. I took the aerial shots and developed them in the laundry out the back of the house in Redfern.

'I made a map of the place and doodled annotations around the side. I knew a bit about what happened at the homes of prominent businessmen on Sunday evenings. The drinks on the terrace in the warmth of the

167

afternoon, inside if it was raining, a barbecue either way, guests leaving around four-thirty in the afternoon, the serious talkers staying on, toasted sandwiches, brandy, doing business. And of course,' she conceded some realism to match my sceptical groans, 'Lily filled me in.

'I didn't want to be seen but I had to be prepared for it. I wore jeans and runners and a thick jumper and a coat with pockets and a scarf. I walked around the waterfront path and climbed up the sandstone steps to the first wall, ducked along it to the right and made the shrubs, the trees beyond, the line of palms and jacaranda along the southern fence, planted to obscure the overlook of the 1960s flats on the subdivide next door.

'I wait, catch my breath. The sun is going down. The guests drift inside and talk in the kitchen area. Lights go on inside. I try the sliding glass doors to the office — there's no light on there yet. I have maybe twenty minutes before Robert retires to his office to do a bit of business with Max or Harry or Larry or a visitor from interstate. In those twenty minutes Robert will brew his favourite coffee and take the pot and a packet of small cigars and the gentlemen to settle into leather lounge chairs. They too are seduced by the aura of safe and respectable, the perfect life.

'I search the office fast, rifle the filing cabinet. Lily Simms has said to look under L for Landscape Gardening, W for Waste Disposal and E for Efficiency.

'The title deeds for the property portfolio are under L. I pack the folder into the lining of my coat and search for the next one. Fumbling. Scrabbling. Arrivals are imminent. Someone is walking along the corridor towards the office door. I stuff the nearest folders into my coat and almost leap out the doorway onto the patio. I stop. Breathe. Re-lock the door behind me.'

Frances Smith stops her story at this point, for applause perhaps. I applaud. Solange offers to make tea. 'Don't go on without me, I want to hear every word,' she calls from the kitchen. I want to ask Frances Smith if she's making it all up. I want to exclaim with amazement and vicarious fear if she isn't. I maintain my relaxed pose and she continues. I recognise the techniques of shock, of control, of being aghast and needing to make the pieces fit.

'The way back was easier, darkness had come and I was protected now by the interior lighting which made the people inside blind to the night outside. I only had to make the sandy edge of the harbour. The tide was coming in and I waded carefully to the edge of the sand and climbed around the rocks to the driveway of the block of flats next door. Those subdivisions in the 1960s had let the riffraff in.'

Solange interrupts Frances: 'No darling, now is not the time for diversions into suburban sociology. Well done and I'm glad you're back but let's see what your little adventure produced.' She pours the tea and Frances Smith spreads the contents of the two folders out around us.

'None of it looks up to much.'

'There are no handy lists of names and addresses of politicians, judges and sporting identities.'

'What about coded messages from Golden Triangle drug suppliers? Or signed confessions or blackmail documents, compromising photos or keys?'

'There's this list of company addresses, directors' names and bank accounts.' Frances Smith passes them across. 'And this folder,' she announces quietly but with confidence, or smugness, pulling a third folder from her coat lining. She announces the contents: 'Land title deeds, loans, guarantors, dates due and interest rates, more bank accounts, a list of overseas companies in the Cayman Islands, Hong Kong and Monaco.'

It is Solange who notices that over half of them are in the name of Lily Simms nee Harris, alias Lillian Thompson alias Lin Stewart alias Tiger Lily Rose.

'Let's just put these title deeds in a safe place,' I say too quickly, trying to appear businesslike. But Frances Smith is faster. 'I'll look after them,' she says, grabbing the sheets of paper together and heading for the door.

CHAPTER 14

It was fascination, I know

It's our fascination with the big man, the powerful man. They have, people tell me, a real charisma, an aura. When they are physically immense, it is a bodily presence. With Robert Simms it is the neatness of his clothes and their flamboyance — hound's-tooth jackets, black and white checks, a yellow tuxedo with a deep blue tie, that white duck suit for the autumn racing carnival, a pale green tie. And with Max it is the close shave from the Redfern Street barber every morning at nine. You could set your watch by him. Harry Bean likes to think it is his fitness, his physical strength, but it's only his proximity. Close to hand. But they all agree, believe, it is the bodily assumptions, the command, the knowledge, that assures success, power. We want them to speak for us, to think, to decide, to explain — everything will be all right.

'The old father figure,' Frances Smith would say. And it looks like that. But a whole country can't be craving a father figure who beat the odds. On our behalf.

CHAPTER 15

A stroke of luck

It is one of those clear warming early spring evenings. I walk along the beach in the full moonlight, let the wind play across my skin, walking the edges of clarity, solution. The tide is very low. I walk around the headlands between the bays, climb over rocks, up and down stone steps, along paths. I have been invited, by Robert, by telephone, on Max's recommendation, to come for a drink on Sunday afternoon. The route of Frances Smith's break-in is available. I take it and consciously give Robert something to link us.

From below the house lights blaze. There are people leaning on the garden wall. I climb the steps and cross the lawn. Robert is sitting at a table on the patio, waiting for me. I take my seat. He offers me a cigarette. I take one and light it. Right in the heart of the beast. In the bowels, Harry would say. I pour a glass of water from the jug which is also waiting. Every movement and gesture is slow, precise, deliberate. I am breathing from deep in my chest. Then I yawn.

'I didn't realise we were almost neighbours.'

I smoke in silence, gathering the time into my body, my lungs, despite the cigarette smoke. My chest expands and expands and I am full of it, time, patience, waiting.

'Would you like a drink?'

'Brandy, thank you.' He gets up and brings the bottle and two glasses. No ice. I get up and get the ice. Moving quickly, as if I am familiar with this place.

I take a sip of the brandy and look back at Robert Simms. His well-kept face is ugly in the contrasts, sharp garden lighting and the dark beyond. The people at the garden wall move inside the house. I can hear the sounds of talking, modulation of voices rising and falling, laughter, long sentences, punch lines.

I say, 'Here's the deal: Louise and Lily out of gaol, leave Harry Bean alone, permanently, and lean off Max — he's disintegrating under the pressure. Early retirement, I think, just a pension, nothing special. Just get him off my back.'

'And in return? What can you do for me Miss Stevens? Free legal advice?' He laughs. I laugh. Ho ho ha ha. I feel sick.

Robert Simms sits and watches the laughter dribble off. 'You are dealing in artefacts, relics, of some value to the scholar perhaps, the historian, but nothing in the market. And I am in the market these days — I may float a public company, try for a listing on the stock exchange. Tax minimisation. There are certain pleasures in working the rules and regulations, when, like I do, you have enough capital and interests to move it around. I am even thinking of retiring.'

I say things like 'evidence' and 'witnesses'. He says, 'You can't break the law to prove a case. We are not in a situation of equal reversal. I can go straight but you can't bend the rules.'

'If there's enough noise . . .' I say, as if thinking out loud. 'Once the talking starts it escalates. There could be another Royal Commission. No. I think there might be enough to go straight to a committal.'

'I'm afraid, Miss Stevens, it is you who are in danger of prosecution. Break and enter. Stolen goods. My reputation is only enhanced by your assertions. Hearsay. And I might say again that which is obtained by illegal means cannot be admitted as evidence.'

173

'Evidence law is changing. Judges are letting a few things in. It depends on the case. There are precedents.' I speak very slowly, breathing after each sentence: 'You had your own brother killed. Max Cavanagh has done enough years on your behalf to fill another lifetime . . .'

'And don't forget your friend Harry. Your evidence, Miss Stevens, won't touch me but it will take your friends down with you.' He snaps his fingers as if to illustrate the ease of their demise. The voices in the kitchen come up, doors open, people wander out into the garden, stand around. A fat man I don't recognise, along with Max and a woman who is probably Susan, Robert's wife.

I've never been a good loser. When backed into a corner I have a tendency to become extremely emotional, make loud speeches. I resort to vitriol and verbal facility, a deranged belief that the very words can make a difference.

'On your feet, Miss Stevens.' It is Max's voice from the doorway.

Robert is leaning back in his chair, friendlier now. 'I'd like my photographs returned, and the rest of the rubbish, if it's not too much trouble. Now you know your way here, you can drop them by any time, on your way home from work, say, six-thirty, tomorrow?'

I am backing towards the garden wall wishing for the first time in my life that I had a gun and knew how to use it. I aim and shoot anyway. 'He's setting you up, Max; it's been him all along.'

We play statues in the garden for a long minute. Max's arm moves across his chest.

'Ask him about Joey and Lily,' I yell. 'He's got statements, statutory declarations from all those guys who say you took Joey out.'

For a moment I think it's going to play exactly and then the fat man steps up to Robert and Susan drifts into a faint and comes up out of it again, all in one motion, taking the attention. The fat man takes another step and his hand is on Max's arm. Robert turns his back on them, bows slightly at Susan. She comes towards me. I feel like I am really going to faint. The brandy warmth leaves me as the panic rises. I crumple at the knees and hold onto the wall.

Max starts shouting, 'Stupid bitch, moron, dilettante,' and I am back, raising an arm towards Susan's attempt to restrain or help me. I grab her wrist, twist the arm up behind her back, neat, a shield. Robert is caught midway between Max and me. I shout back: 'The fat man can't fight to save his mother, Max. You're gone from this outfit anyway . . . go on, help me.'

There is a sudden silence and a thump. The fat man falls solidly to the ground then rises to his knees like he knows he should be doing something. Max chops fast to that place beneath the skull, the fat man sighs and groans into unconsciousness. Max has his gun out, waving it from Robert to Susan and me and back again.

Susan and I begin a sideways crab-walk in a wide circle. The gun stays on Robert. We all breathe out heavily and start talking at once.

'In the study, bottom right — two guns. Bottom left —' I say as Max throws me a gun— 'negatives and photographs.' I catch the gun and run, still talking: 'Blackmail material, tapes. The safe deposit key is in the crystal vase.' Max comes out with a gun in each hand. 'Let's go. Now,' I say, with immense fake authority.

'You get the stuff,' Max orders as he advances on Robert.

I throw the packets and bundles into a briefcase standing open on the desk and race back out in time to see Robert fall to his knees. I wish Frances were here to capture the greatest shot of the decade. It's a grubby and unsophisticated scene. Max swings his right leg back and high like a footballer making the deciding attempt . . . The kneeling god splays backwards into the garden pond, sinking, taking in water. Susan stands her ground and I yell, 'Now, come on, search her,' and 'I don't know the way out.'

Max grabs Susan and we stumble through the house to alarming sounds of the fat man coming round, a thrashing of water. We race for the garage, the remote controls, and doors swing up like magic to free a pair of BMWs.

'I'll take the sedan, you can have the sports.' I am puffing with exertion and fear. I fling the briefcase across the roof at him and concentrate hard on the car, screeching in reverse and swinging into Vaucluse Road. I drive like a car thief, fast and serious down the S-bends into Rose Bay and Double Bay and on into the inner city and somewhere safer than being alone. All the way to Redfern I try to make myself believe that Robert Simms was going to kill me.

CHAPTER 16

Natural causes

Anne Stevens came into the house fast and efficient. She was all geared up. Solange and I instinctively backed into far-apart chairs. She began quite calmly: 'Something terrible has happened. It wasn't my fault but I think there's going to be trouble, real trouble, police trouble.' By the end of the sentence she was breathless. Panting.

Solange went off to make a cup of tea. The telephone rang and she answered it in the kitchen. I kept one ear on the cadence of her voice and the other on Stevens' rising panic.

'Murder,' she was saying 'I could hear him drowning.'

'Heart attack,' said Solange, coming in with a tea tray and fruit cake. 'It's all fixed.' She explained to Anne: 'That was Harry on the phone. He'll come by and pick you up in an hour or two. Sugar? Yes, I think so — for shock.' I took Lily at face value and Anne Stevens with a grain of salt but I never underestimated Solange.

CHAPTER 17

What to do about Max

If he was young he'd be part of the live-fast-die-young Joey Simms' life but he's middle-aged and facing the second phase of danger. Instead, takeover, fall guy, handy sap — someone has to take the fall and Max Cavanagh makes an exemplary arrest.

They say if you make it to fifty they leave you alone. Max is in gaol again and he's at least fifty-five. The police have him on hand for questioning at any time. They want him to make another deal, finger someone, set up someone else. They offer this and he declines. I ask him why he doesn't leave the country and he says he has no-one to make the arrangements, that no-one in the world will talk to him, that he's alone, like a leper. I don't believe this.

Max is on the answer phone. I ring back. He's left the police cells. On his way to Long Bay. I set off out there. I go through the depositions with him, many statements backed up, tight, a good array of physical evidence, a neat little basket of bullshit. Who can tell?

I take the files home with me every night and go into the office on Sundays. I work out a possible strategy. I go out to Long Bay to see Max. 'It's three weeks before we are on,' I say, hoping this deadline will concentrate his mind. 'You'd be better off with a QC, someone with a high profile. You're going to need the press this time. I don't suppose you've got a friend in forensic?'

'No. No friends.' Max is dispirited and I might be moved by him if it weren't for the body of history. The bodies. I leave him with a couple of packets of cigarettes and a lot to worry about.

Although Robert Simms' death should have made a difference the charges against Max were too far along to decorously hinder or abandon proceedings. But the fire had gone out of the witnesses and the prosecution was less than hungry. He had his eye on the big cases and this one had turned into small fry.

And with Robert Simms no longer around to deliver the pay-off and the succession in limbo, we simply went through the motions. I made a neat cross-examination and a thoroughly professional, almost eminent summation based on cases and on law. I liked myself again after that. I had been able to play the game through to its legalistic end.

FIRST ENDING

Across town the thin man is at lunch at the art gallery restaurant. Down on the beach the fat man is walking in socks and sandals for exercise, to meet someone.

Anne Stevens comes up off the sand and tell Frances and Solange that the fat man is taking his stomach for a walk down there. They all rush to the cliff top and peer over, watching him watch his children as they swim out on the small waves and float back yelling daddy daddy did you see me surf.

These small scenes makes us forget and remember. Every town has its fat man and its thin man. They rarely speak to each other, entirely a nodding acquaintance, move in different circles, never go to the same places, but their timing is exquisite, their movements like a long-distance dance that holds a city in its hands, squeezing, wringing every last drop of cash or kudos from the grip. The thin man thinks he's a thinker and the fat man just thinks rich. They own things — clout,

179

connections, accountants, things that shore up the edges of the public, the news, the discourse, the tone of voice. They do not pay attention to music. They do not sing.

The day comes grey and wintry with the wind building to a gale. The newspaper slaps against the front door and the smell of coffee is a lesser pleasure in the wake of sex and you still here. What day is it? Monday. What's going on?

Harry says, 'How much do you know about Frances Smith?'

Anne laughs, 'She's my best friend, mate. Don't even think about it.'

All morning they drink coffee and get in each other's way and try, again and again, to begin the conversation that is going to make it all right. How to unravel the knot they have become.

He says, 'Remember when it was all just a romantic accident?' and she says 'I don't remember it like that,' and he says 'When somebody is important . . . Do you know we are important to each other?' and she unplugs the telephone and sits very still in the armchair and stares out the window at the rain that has come down like a shroud over the land.

Anne, Solange, Anthony and I assemble for a fine evening. We drink, dance, we play seven card stud on the dining room table until it is late enough to go out. Card games are social occasions for the acting out of varieties of aggression. I win and decide to skip the late-night outing and catch a cab home. Harry Bean drops by two hours later. Suddenly I feel like going out, being in company, free of intimacy. We meet up with the others at Le Bar. Anthony and Anne dance, she in a spiv's tuxedo and he in his Italian drape suit, silk shirt, brogues.

Harry shakes his head, his eyes glued on Anthony. 'They look like a couple of poofters,' he says desperately.

'They look like a couple of gangsters to me,' I say, 'but they're only lawyers dancing.'

He turns to give me his attention, 'All those other stories . . .' he begins. The head-shaking has become a sort of pathetic habit.

'What's troubling you, Harry? I mean really.'

'All those stories,' he says again, 'going on . . .' I guess he's drunk or stoned or something — he is certainly not his old self. I am a bit tipsy, in no mood for the serious stuff. 'Did she tell you she was kidnapped?' I say, lightening the tone.

'She told me a lot of things,' he replies.

'But what we have to remember are the bits that never happened,' I say.

'Exactly,' Harry brightens up. He and I are on the same wavelength. 'That's exactly what you do have to remember. All the things that never happened. Very profound, Miss Smith.' He laughs, I can almost see the transformation spread through his body — he is returning to himself from somewhere a long way away. I know exactly how that feels. 'It could have been worse,' we chorus together.

Frances and Solange come across each other in the street late in the afternoon. Solange is hurrying and Frances is there on the footpath smiling at her concentration.

'Oh,' she says, 'there you are. I was just going in here to buy some flowers. Here, a bunch of eleven red roses, breaking the habit.'

In the city street, anonymity. They talk about beach pollution, theatre reviewers and skin cream. Other stories going on.

CHAPTER 18

A few clues

I appeared for Max. He got off. Again. I went into exhaustion. That state of panic and shock — you have been so tired for so long that you think it is normal. A glass or two of wine and I was cranky drunk. A setback at the bank and I was full-flight angry. The tellers and the managers would bring out their full range of anti-customer techniques — telling you what you already know, saying over and over again, it can't be done. I'd reply with one of my old lines: 'If I was a drug runner you'd manage to do it in a flash. Or a corporate high-flyer,' I'd add. I'd been reading the papers again. This was a sign of normality. I was relishing the corporate high-flyers poised on the precipice. The Stock Exchange crashed and I was disappointed there were no suicides.

'It's an insult to the garden to call them tall poppies,' I muttered. 'I like to think of them as privet trees — no cutting back ever gets rid of them and every spring, when the seed flowers are made, when the company reports come in, they cause ordinary people to sneeze and drip, the image of discomfort, of powerlessness against the urban elements.' When I lost my temper at the bank it was Max's cheque I was trying to get cleared.

The electricity had been cut off — I'd gone vague and failed to pay the bill. I had failed to buy more candles, had spent the last money on a litre bottle of red wine bought with surprise and pleasure, crossing the suburbs to find it, the memory of Italy, reliving the past, the beginning, going back, going back to get out of the present. It doesn't work, never has, but a litre of wine will make it bearable for a few days.

And then suddenly it was over, I was recovered, the bottle only half drunk at the end of the week, enough sleep. Perhaps the past does work its medicine. Each day I walked from Watsons Bay to Bondi along the cliff tops in the wind, and back again, filling in time, pacing out the anxiety, making the present into the past by endurance, splendid views and clear air. The despair crystallised: I had won in court and somehow lost in life, on the moral front. I'd become willingly involved in a master narrative that could only make me peripheral, complicit. The walking helped. The words, even concise and grand words, did not make the difference.

It always seems mysterious when you turn that final corner back to optimism. It was summer, of course. Daylight saving and the long days stretching to free the body. Vera rang with another of her grand plans and another change of address.

My cousin Mary Stevens rang out of the blue. We met for coffee in Darlinghurst. I wondered if I would recognise her. The coffee shop was old, worn out now with the years of always being there with the best brew in the city. She sat inside the front window near the phone, her diary open, a pile of twenty and ten cent coins, doing business.

I smiled and nodded to her. She looked a little like my father around the eyes. She nodded back and gestured at the pile of coins. 'Car phone's on the blink,' she said, and turned her attention to me, ordered another cup of coffee, asked me what I would have and said, 'I've been hearing stories about you.'

It was awkward. A public place and perched on stools at a counter, not a place for grand family talk. Perhaps there was nothing to say. Read any good books lately?

I settle for the easy social, 'What are you doing these days?'

'I've moved up to Sydney, for work. I do a bit of everything these days, administration, organising, driving.' She is looking past me through the plate-glass window. I follow her gaze — a good dark grey Mercedes, black windows, interstate numberplates. I look suitably impressed. Perhaps she works for a politician or a diplomat. Then she said, 'I see your friend Max got his the other day, an OD in a hotel room. Did you know he used?'

'He didn't,' I say quickly to cover my astonishment at the turn in the conversation.

'That's what they all say.'

'It's a common enough thing, murder by heroin overdose.'

'All your fine work wasted.'

'At least I had the cheque cashed before he went. Could have been one of a hundred people. He had a lot of enemies.'

'You know who it was.'

It wasn't a question. I wanted to say I didn't do it and then remembered my father's fantasy about taking the fella out into the bush and putting a gun to his head. We lack courage and the desire to be known as killers. I was not a suspect. Although I cannot say I wasn't relieved.

'You do know who did it. Think.'

The exhilaration returned to my body, that feeling when you don't know what you think until you start speaking. The act of speech, the forever mysterious link between language and meaning — I began talking about the last time I had seen Max.

'We left the court-room together. After the third not

185

guilty they couldn't really hold him on anything else. We went down in the lift together and out into the crisp spring sunshine. We stood in Macquarie Street for a minute or two. I sensed he was waiting for something, someone, and we made small talk for the public view. The press were there but in the distance — his was an old story or a story told once too often to be news. He handed me the envelope containing the cheque and said, "I was always confident you would do the right thing by me," but if we had lost he would have torn the cheque into pieces and fluttered it out the window of the prison van.

'I took the cheque out and checked the amount, the date, the signature. It was for fifty thousand dollars. He said, "I told you I was generous." I put the cheque in the inside pocket of my suit and we stood together in public silence. I had not been dismissed. He was waiting for someone and I guessed he did not want to be standing there alone. Pride, I thought at the time — he wants always to be publicly accompanied. Security too, I supposed, but pride was the big thing. His fabulous suits, the crisp cotton shirts, his slightly bulging forehead covered with a perfect haircut.

'A car drove up and tooted its horn. It was a small BMW, one of the new ones. A woman in sunglasses, hat and gloves looked straight at us. He moved towards the car without saying another word and I turned, my own pride in play, to walk away. As he opened the car door the woman at the wheel continued to look at me. I felt rather than saw this. I looked back. She raised her sunglasses to the brim of her hat, in preparation for a kiss, I thought, and now see it as a characteristic gesture, one I had seen before. But I didn't get it. Not then.

'Weeks later I woke up in a great panic, sweating and moaning and grasping for the slipped image of the dream that had disturbed me. Something I had missed.

'I knew the woman in the car,' I say to Mary Stevens. 'She had intended me to know her. That gesture of putting her sunglasses up on top of her head, on to the brim of her hat, and then chatting on until the hour was up and then, always, extending the hour by searching her bag, her person, the room, for her glasses, which were still on her head, in plain sight, and I would never tell her this, which was exactly the point of the exercise. It was the only time she ever tested me.

'It was Lily, of course. Changed. In disguise. I didn't want to know it was her. It would have made me sick. Perhaps it did. I had an awful three months after that trial.'

Mary Stevens didn't respond to my revelation. She nodded at me to go on and I said, 'There's nothing more to tell. It was probably Lily who killed him. She had that sort of courage and a lot of moral righteousness.'

'She had a lot of reasons, sure, and years to act on them, sure. So why now?'

'How do you know all this?' I ask, thrown by the specificity of her questions, the intimate knowledge of our neatly buried adventures.

'You do not think that you have been unobserved?' she says. 'You don't think you could have got away with it if it hadn't been in someone's interest?'

I give up. 'Enough talking in riddles. The chapter is closed,' I say, feeling both ridiculous and powerful. 'How would you know what goes on in this town?' I am rising angry. 'You've only just got here.'

CHAPTER 19

Frances has the last word

I thought I'd made it clear that I couldn't be trusted. I talked about the past. I didn't talk about the past. I revealed secrets. I kept secrets. I took the city at face value, lived on the surface, found a place to be if not safe then safe enough. Risks. Rushes. Love and danger keep you free. I saw the city as a maze — hide, disguise, leave, arrive, the rest is not my business. I imagined I'd done just fine. Just? Enough? I argued with myself. I was convinced. I am, after all, the daughter of Frank Smith. I was born knowing the facts as well as the fictions.

And now a messenger arrives at my house. She climbs the wide stairway to the lounge room where I sit with the afternoon sun streaming in the window. We shake hands. Her name is Mary. She says, 'Your father's an old man. He wants to meet with you, one last time.'

I acquiesce. I go across the suburbs in the back seat of a large car. I step into the hotel foyer and take the lift to the penthouse suite. I reach out to open the door and it opens for me. Lily stands to the side of the doorway and smiles at me, a greeting, 'Hello Frances, we are so pleased you came.'

I am not speechless. I just choose not to speak. I go into the great room full of light and blasted with harbour views and the sound of the television set in another room. The sun goes down as I watch it and my father talks his message of forgiveness, acceptance, warning, promise. The announcement that he is taking over in Sydney and doesn't want me interfering. Do I hear the cold threat of it? I suggest he writes me a large cheque.

Lily comes down in the lift with me and we stand in the hotel lobby as my brothers, Arch and Leon, hunk their way through the revolving door, looking all around them like hoods in a Brecht play, caricatures. They see me, or rather they see Lily and walk towards her and then they see me and slow down. Their bulk gives them a momentum that makes quick halts in casual stride difficult. For big men they are surprisingly clumsy on their large flat feet.

I smile hellos to Arch and Leon and they forget their tough-strangers-in-a-new-city wariness and greet me like a kid sister. For a moment I regret the cheque in my pocket and the loneliness. Arch and Leon have nice wives and many children and they tell me about them. Brett's in high school and Lucinda's going to university after Christmas and little Matthew's had another operation on his legs and should be walking by Easter. Bubby's starting at kindergarten and Petal is a really good rider. 'Like you were,' says Leon, touching my sense of loss.

Lily hovers at the edges of this banal chat, as if we might let something slip that threatens her position with my father. They all but ignore her, claiming their own family as a buffer against her brittle and ruthless business. I step away from her, going towards the door, and they fall in beside me.

'If you came back — ' Arch starts.

'We could work together,' Leon continues.

I look at them, turning my head from side to side as if I am watching a tennis match. Lily is standing a yard or two behind us, immobile, completely calm. I turn the turning of my head into a shake, answering their offer in the negative. We put our arms around each other and give each other a big hug and start laughing, like kids again. 'She's only mortal,' I say into Leon's shoulder and Arch says, 'Is that an order?'

'No,' I say, stepping back from the embrace. 'She's good at her job and she'll look after the business well. You wouldn't be here without her and if it wasn't you it would be someone else. You might be my brothers but that doesn't mean I like you.' The moment of warmth has passed. I leave them and go out the revolving door, taking it a full turn, like a clown, having one last word: 'Don't go out in the sun without a hat on,' I say. 'It can get hot out there.'

And then I'm gone, out into the burning smelly street with the cars tearing up to the Cross as if they are all in a chase scene on TV. I walk the other way, towards the city. When in doubt, see a movie — *My Beautiful Laundrette* — and walk up Pitt Street to Central and through the park behind it. I make a booking at the tennis court on the way home and ring Stevens to see if she wants a game.

END NOTES

On rare occasions Lily would tell her favourite bit of the story: 'Robert assumed I'd sign them over for a reasonable price but I wouldn't, so a week later I get arrested for passing dud cheques and end up in Mulawa for six months with this crazy sane friend of yours also in for cheques or something. I never could work out her story. She had this book of yours. It had your name and address so primly in it, with all your pompous qualifications neatly printed after it, dated, the works. I even remember the date, July 16, 1979. Some big deal for you, was it, buying *The Interpretation of Dreams*? We all read it and talked about it — it was readable, I'll give you that — and we all stopped taking tranquillisers and started having great dreams. I can tell you, it helped pass the time.'

Vera and I talk on the phone once or twice a week. She still has the children, still works like a demon, has clocked up a year in lieu and still there's never enough time. She sends me cases of fresh fruit and cuttings from the local papers, horror stories made intimate by place, proximity. I am relieved when she gets a dog, an Alsatian cross that found her and stayed. Once she showed me her double-barrelled shotgun on top of the wardrobe. She says you can't live in fear and I say you can't live without it and either of us could have said either sentence.

I often wake in the night from the sounds of gunshots. Dreaming. For if the truth is told, most gunshots, apart from police raids, are in broad daylight.

191

Harry says there are at least two versions of what happened that night. A spurned lover (Ruth) crashed the family serenity, making a scene. And a rampaging dope fiend robbed the place and held the family hostage. Both scenarios precipitated Robert's heart attack and subsequent drowning. We say that this is poetic justice, it being the only sort of justice available these days.

About the Author

Jan McKemmish was born in Australia in 1950. She grew up on a dairy farm. She later moved to Sydney, where she worked as a teacher, cook, journalist and writer. She has received grants from the Literature Board of the Australia Council and has been a guest of writers festivals throughout Australia. *A Gap in the Records*, her first novel, was published to wide acclaim in 1985 and is now considered a cult classic that exploded the stylistic limits of the spy thriller genre. She is working on a third novel, *Common Knowledge*.

Books from Cleis Press

FICTION

Another Love by Erzsébet Galgóczi.
ISBN: 0-939416-52-2 24.95 cloth; ISBN: 0-939416-51-4 8.95 paper.

Cosmopolis: Urban Stories by Women edited by Ines Rieder.
ISBN: 0-939416-36-0 24.95 cloth; ISBN: 0-939416-37-9 9.95 paper.

A Forbidden Passion by Cristina Peri Rossi.
ISBN: 0-939416-64-0 24.95 cloth; ISBN: 0-939416-68-9 9.95 paper.

In the Garden of Dead Cars by Sybil Claiborne.
ISBN: 0-939416-65-4 24.95 cloth; ISBN: 0-939416-66-2 9.95 paper.

Night Train To Mother by Ronit Lentin.
ISBN: 0-939416-29-8 24.95 cloth; ISBN: 0-939416-28-X 9.95 paper.

The One You Call Sister: New Women's Fiction
edited by Paula Martinac.
ISBN: 0-939416-30-1 24.95 cloth; ISBN: 0-939416031-X 9.95 paper.

Only Lawyers Dancing by Jan McKemmish
ISBN: 0-939416-70-0 24.95 cloth; ISBN: 0-939416-69-7 9.95 paper

Unholy Alliances: New Women's Fiction edited by Louise Rafkin.
ISBN: 0-939416-14-X 21.95 cloth; ISBN: 0-939416-15-8 9.95 paper.

The Wall by Marlen Haushofer.
ISBN: 0-939416-53-0 24.95 cloth; ISBN: 0-939416-54-9 paper.

LATIN AMERICA

**Beyond the Border: A New Age in Latin American Women's
Fiction** edited by Nora Erro-Peralta and Caridad Silva-Núñez.
ISBN: 0-939416-42-5 24.95 cloth; ISBN: 0-939416-43-3 12.95 paper.

**The Little School: Tales of Disappearance and Survival
in Argentina** by Alicia Partnoy.
ISBN: 0-939416-08-5 21.95 cloth; ISBN: 0-939416-07-7 9.95 paper.

Revenge of the Apple by Alicia Partnoy.
ISBN: 0-939416-62-X 24.95 cloth; ISBN: 0-939416-63-8 8.95 paper.

You Can't Drown the Fire: Latin American Women Writing in Exile edited by Alicia Partnoy.
ISBN: 0-939416-16-6 24.95 cloth; ISBN: 0-939416-17-4 9.95 paper.

AUTOBIOGRAPHY, BIOGRAPHY, LETTERS

Peggy Deery: An Irish Family at War by Nell McCafferty.
ISBN: ISBN: 0-939416-38-7 24.95 cloth; ISBN: 0-939416-39-5 9.95 paper.

The Shape of Red: Insider/Outsider Reflections by Ruth Hubbard and Margaret Randall.
ISBN: 0-939416-19-0 24.95 cloth; ISBN: 0-939416-18-2 9.95 paper.

Women & Honor: Some Notes on Lying by Adrienne Rich.
ISBN: 0-939416-44-1 3.95 paper.

ANIMAL RIGHTS

And a Deer's Ear, Eagle's Song and Bear's Grace: Relationships Between Animals and Women edited by Theresa Corrigan and Stephanie T. Hoppe.
ISBN: 0-939416-38-7 24.95 cloth; ISBN: 0-939416-39-5 9.95 paper.

With a Fly's Eye, Whale's Wit and Woman's Heart: Relationships Between Animals and Women edited by Theresa Corrigan and Stephanie T. Hoppe.
ISBN: 0-939416-24-7 24.95 cloth; ISBN: 0-939416-25-5 9.95 paper.

POLITICS OF HEALTH

The Absence of the Dead Is Their Way of Appearing by Mary Winfrey Trautmann. ISBN: 0-939416-04-2 8.95 paper.

AIDS: The Women edited by Ines Rieder and Patricia Ruppelt.
ISBN: 0-939416-20-4 24.95 cloth; ISBN: 0-939416-21-2 9.95 paper

Don't: A Woman's Word by Elly Danica.
ISBN: 0-939416-23-9 21.95 cloth; ISBN: 0-939416-22-0 8.95 paper

1 in 3: Women with Cancer Confront an Epidemic edited by Judith Brady.
ISBN: 0-939416-50-6 24.95 cloth; ISBN: 0-939416-49-2 10.95 paper.

Voices in the Night: Women Speaking About Incest
edited by Toni A.H. McNaron and Yarrow Morgan.
ISBN: 0-939416-02-6 9.95 paper.

With the Power of Each Breath: A Disabled Women's Anthology
edited by Susan Browne, Debra Connors and Nanci Stern.
ISBN: 0-939416-09-3 24.95 cloth; ISBN: 0-939416-06-9 10.95 paper.

Woman-Centered Pregnancy and Birth
by the Federation of Feminist Women's Health Centers.
ISBN: 0-939416-03-4 11.95 paper.

LESBIAN STUDIES

Boomer: Railroad Memoirs by Linda Niemann.
ISBN: 0-939416-55-7 12.95 paper.

Different Daughters: A Book by Mothers of Lesbians
edited by Louise Rafkin.
ISBN: 0-939416-12-3 21.95 cloth; ISBN: 0-939416-13-1 9.95 paper.

*Different Mothers: Sons & Daughters of Lesbians Talk
About Their Lives* edited by Louise Rafkin.
ISBN: 0-939416-40-9 24.95 cloth; ISBN: 0-939416-41-7 9.95 paper.

A Lesbian Love Advisor by Celeste West.
ISBN: 0-939416-27-1 24.95 cloth; ISBN: 0-939416-26-3 9.95 paper.

*Long Way Home: The Odyssey of a Lesbian Mother
and Her Children* by Jeanne Jullion. ISBN: 0-939416-05-0 8.95 paper.

More Serious Pleasure: Lesbian Erotic Stories and Poetry
edited by the Sheba Collective.
ISBN: 0-939416-48-4 24.95 cloth; ISBN: 0-939416-47-6 9.95 paper.

The Night Audrey's Vibrator Spoke: A Stonewall Riots Collection
by Andrea Natalie. ISBN: 0-939416-64-6 8.95 paper.

Queer and Pleasant Danger: Writing Out My Life
by Louise Rafkin. ISBN: 0-939416-60-3 24.95 cloth; ISBN: 0-939416-61-1 9.95 paper.

Serious Pleasure: Lesbian Erotic Stories and Poetry
edited by the Sheba Collective.
ISBN: 0-939416-46-8 24.95 cloth; ISBN: 0-939416-45-X 9.95 paper.

SEXUAL POLITICS

Good Sex: Real Stories from Real People by Julia Hutton.
ISBN: 0-939416-56-5 24.95 cloth; ISBN: 0-939416-57-3 12.95 paper.

Madonnarama: Essays on Sex and Popular Culture
edited by Lisa Frank and Paul Smith.
ISBN: 0-939416-72-7 24.95 cloth; ISBN: 0-939416-71-9 9.95 paper.

Sex Work: Writings by Women in the Sex Industry
edited by Frédérique Delacoste and Priscilla Alexander.
ISBN: 0-939416-10-7 24.95 cloth; ISBN: 0-939416-11-5 16.95 paper.

Susie Bright's Sexual Reality: A Virtual Sex World Reader
by Susie Bright. ISBN: 0-939416-58-1 24.95 cloth; ISBN: 0-939416-59-X 9.95 paper.

Susie Sexpert's Lesbian Sex World by Susie Bright.
ISBN: 0-939416-34-4 24.95 cloth; ISBN: 0-939416-35-2 9.95 paper.

Since 1980, Cleis Press has published progressive books by women.
We welcome your order and will ship your books as quickly as
possible. Individual orders must be prepaid (U.S. dollars only).
Please add 15% shipping. Pennsylvania residents add 6% sales tax.
Mail orders: Cleis Press, P.O. Box 8933, Pittsburgh, Pennsylvania
15221. **MasterCard and Visa orders:** include account number,
expiration date, and signature. Fax your credit card order to (412)
937-1567 or telephone us Monday through Friday, 9am–5pm EST,
at (412) 937-1555.